The Whole Nine Yarns

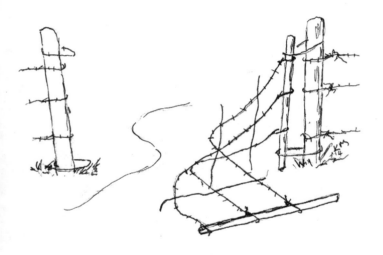

Tales of the West

The Whole Nine Yarns

Tales of the West

Jim Moore

 Raven Publishing, Inc.
Norris, MT

The Whole Nine Yarns: Tales of the West
Copyright © 2014 Jim Moore
Gate illustrations, pages 1 and 142 © 2014 Kay Moore

Published by Raven Publishing, Inc.
PO Box 2866, Norris, MT 59745

ISBN: 978-1-937849-22-1

The stories in this book are works of fiction. The similarity of the characters or events depicted in these stories to any person or situation is coincidental.

Library of Congress Cataloging-in-Publication Data

Moore, Jim, 1927-
 The whole nine yarns : tales of the West / Jim Moore.
    pages cm
 ISBN 978-1-937849-22-1 (paperback : alk. paper)
 1. Western stories. I. Title.
 PS3613.O5626W46 2014
 813'.6--dc23
                                2014011043

For Kay — as always

The Whole Nine Yarns

Tales of the West

Nine Short Stories
by Jim Moore

THE PROPOSAL

It was Ruby who insisted the men build the log school and the smaller teacherage, tucked away in the willow brush out of the wind. Ruby, too, found Miss Uremovich and persuaded her to come to that lonely place to teach the seven children who made up the student body.

Miss Uremovich was tall, almost six feet tall. She wore shapeless black dresses that concealed her figure—if she had a figure. Her face was plain, framed by dark hair, pulled back and tied in a bun at her neck. The glasses she wore had thick lenses that made her eyes appear to be twice as large as normal. She was quiet of manner and distant in her relationship with the few others who lived in that tiny community, lost in cattle country. Her age was a matter of speculation.

Ruby thought she was a good teacher, and Ruby was the only one in Stage Stop who cared about education or cared about Miss Uremovich. Only Ruby visited the teacher at the school or at the teacherage. If Miss Uremovich had a friend, it was Ruby. To the rest of the populace of the town she was just "the schoolmarm."

Stage Stop was appropriately named. It was just a place where the stage came to a halt twice a week on its round trip from White Sulphur Springs to Big Timber. Standing by the road was a hotel that had a dining room on the ground floor, three rooms to rent on the second floor, and living quarters hitched onto the back. The saloon, a long, low log building, stood next to the hotel. On the other side of the road was a small store and post office where the stage loaded and discharged passengers and mail. Two houses, one behind the store, the other next to the creek, made up the rest of the town.

Ruby and her husband were the proprietors of the hotel. Ruby had been a teacher herself before she married Hank and allowed him to drag her away from home and family to the wilds of the Montana Territory. Aside from Miss Uremovich, Ruby had only Chastity for female companionship.

Unlike the town, Chastity was not appropriately named. She tended bar while Rast, to whom she may or may not have been married, helped the customers drink. Chastity was of indeterminate age, wore clothing that Ruby thought scandalous, used language that burned Ruby's ears, and was careless with her favors to the cowpunchers who frequented the saloon.

Those who drank were the denizens of the ranch country around Stage Stop. They generally came to the saloon one at a time or in pairs. Now and again, a large group of those who rode the neighboring ranges would all arrive in town at the same time. Then the night became exciting for them and for Chastity. They drank and gambled. Once in a while she danced with a celebrant to a tune ground out of a violin by Rast, who thought he played like a virtuoso. But most of her time was spent pouring out the whiskey and watching as the men got drunk. As soon as they were drunk enough, she extracted extra money from them when they threw their coins on the bar. Some of it went to Rast. Most she kept for herself.

One Saturday night in the fall of the year, a dozen cowboys from ranches in the valley arrived at the saloon at the same time. After the boys had been drinking for a while and had worn out every other topic of conversation, their talk turned to the schoolmarm. Someone mentioned that she wasn't married. Another wondered why. That led to a discussion about her lonely situation. Soon Silent Clyde, so named because even his whisper could be heard a mile away, backed up against the bar and proclaimed for all to hear, "It's a shame that poor woman doesn't have a husband. I think we have an obligation to remedy the situation. Let's draw straws to decide who goes to the teacherage, knocks on the door, and proposes marriage to Miss Uremovich."

This bit of idiocy stirred up raucous laughter from the inebriated crowd, but they all agreed to abide by the draw, whatever the result. If the cowboys' fogged-up minds allowed them to think about it at all, each was sure another would pull the short straw.

Chastity, entering into the fun, jerked straws from a broom. She carefully broke them all to the same length, broke one in half, and waved the bundle in the air for the bachelors to see. Then she concealed them in her hand for the draw.

One after the other, the punchers stepped forward and pulled a straw from Chastity's fist. Each of the first five to run the risk breathed out a sigh of relief and then giggled when he found that the straw he had pulled was a long one. The sixth to draw was Lawrence, who then stood staring at his hand. That hand held the short straw. At the look on his face, laughter broke out, loud and uproarious. The drunken assembly had found its goat.

Lawrence worked for Anson Gross. He was about nineteen years old, tall and skinny. His forehead sloped back from his eyebrows to a hairline that was already beginning to recede, and his nose hooked down toward a thin mouth above a receding chin. Lawrence was not good looking. He generally kept to himself and never had much to say. His fellow cowpunchers didn't think he was very bright.

The unlucky cowboy was only in the saloon because his employer offered to buy drinks for the crew. They were celebrating the fact that the last of the hay had been pitched onto the stack. Now he was the center of attention with his drunken comrades slapping him on the back and yelling congratulations to him on his good luck. After that activity lost its attraction, they began to speculate on the teacher's reaction to the proposal. It was the consensus that she would slap Lawrence in the face. The prospect of poor Lawrence enduring such a fate caused more laughter and the need for more whiskey.

Lawrence was sober. He had downed only one drink and participated in the drawing only because he couldn't think of a way to avoid it. Now he realized that participation obligated him to propose to Miss Uremovich. There was no way out of it, but there was no fun in it for Lawrence.

The whole gang poured out the door of the saloon, whooping and laughing as they started up the road toward the teacherage, three hundred yards to the west. About halfway there, the ringleader waved them to a stop and directed all but Lawrence to stay out of sight. As Lawrence plodded on up the middle of the road by himself, the others skulked around in the brush to avoid being seen. But all made sure they were close enough to hear the proposal. The rowdies thought they were being quiet, but their noise was so loud it could be heard at the Gross ranch, a mile up the creek.

Lawrence stopped on the path in front of the teacherage, took a deep breath, then stepped to the door and knocked twice. He heard Miss Uremovich walking across the room and just had time to snatch his hat from his head before he was facing her.

She looked him up and down and asked, "Yes?"

Lawrence took a deep breath, gulped, and then asked in return, "Ma'am, will you marry me?"

The conspirators, hidden in the brush, snickered as they listened and then quieted down to hear the reply. Miss Uremovich was silent for only a moment and then said, "You've been drinking, sir, haven't you?" It was more of a statement than a question.

Lawrence looked at his boots and mumbled, "Yes, Ma'am."

"Well, never mind. The answer is yes."

Lawrence didn't know what he had expected, but he certainly hadn't expected her to say yes. Eyebrows lifted in surprise, he mumbled again, "Beg your pardon, Ma'am?"

"I said yes. You asked me to marry you, and I said yes." Then she added, "What's your name, sir?"

"I'm Lawrence McManus, Ma'am." He almost choked when he spoke.

"Mr. McManus, tomorrow is Sunday. You will be sober on Sunday, won't you?"

Lawrence looked at the floor and bobbed his head up and down.

"Well, sir, you return here tomorrow at two o'clock, when you're sober, and we'll discuss the arrangements for the wedding." She started to close the door, then stopped and added, "And please bathe and have on some clean clothes. You do have some clean clothes, don't you?"

When Lawrence nodded, she said, "Good night, sir. We'll set the date for the wedding tomorrow." Then Lawrence found himself staring at the closed door.

While the drunken crowd escorted their newly engaged comrade back down the street to the saloon, their whooping, yelling, and laughing was even louder and more raucous than before. Their foolish scheme had worked even better than they hoped. Back at the saloon, Chastity joined the fun by reminding Lawrence of the obligations of a gentleman. He must marry the woman now that he had proposed and she had accepted. And the whole sotted crowd echoed that he couldn't argue with Chastity. She was a woman, and women knew about such things. Lawrence took the haranguing as long as he could bear it and then escaped out the door and headed for the ranch. On the way, he upchucked beside the trail.

Ruby heard about the escapade the next morning from bleary-eyed Chastity. She wasted no time trudging up the road to the teacherage.

"You said you'd marry Lawrence? Why in the world would you do that?"

A touch of a smile crossed the teacher's lips. "Why not? He and the others were drunk."

Ruby stared at her for a moment, and then leaned back and howled with laughter. "I see what you're up to. They wanted to embarrass you, and you're turning the tables on 'em. You'll let it go on for a while before you tell that boy you could never marry a worthless cowpuncher like him." The laughing stopped and a conspiratorial look appeared on Ruby's face. "What can I do to help?"

"Why, you can help with the wedding. Lawrence—I guess I can call him Lawrence since we're engaged to be married—will be here to decide on the wedding date this afternoon. We'll need a preacher. And we'll need a nice place for the ceremony. The whole drunken bunch that was with Lawrence last night should be put to work shining up the lobby of your hotel."

Ruby rocked in her chair as she laughed some more. "How far are you going to go with this? When will you let 'em know the joke's on them?"

The smile on Miss Uremovich's face broadened a little, but all she said was, "Let it be a surprise."

****

When Lawrence knocked on the door at two o'clock, his hair was slicked back, and his shirt and denim pants were clean. Miss Uremovich led him to a chair and gestured for him to sit. She took a chair opposite, ran her hands down her skirt as though to remove wrinkles, then looked him directly in the eye, and said, "My name is Myrtle Uremovich. From now on you should call me Myrtle, and I'll call you Lawrence." She paused, but Lawrence just sat with his eyes on the floor, so she continued. "Now, we must plan the wedding. I suggest we get married two weeks from yesterday. That's Saturday, the second of October. Will that be all right with you?"

Lawrence, with his arms hanging down between his knees, swallowed hard. When he spoke, it was nearly a whisper. "Yes, Ma'am."

"Lawrence, we're about to become husband and wife. You should call me Myrtle."

"Yes, Ma'am—Myrtle."

"I'll write to the Methodist minister in Big Timber and ask him to be here for the ceremony. Is that all right?"

"Yes, Ma'am."

"The hotel is the only decent building, so the wedding should be there. I'm sure Ruby will agree. Do you agree?"

Lawrence didn't move.

"Ruby will stand up with me. Who do you want to be the best man?"

Lawrence thought hard. "Why, Anson Gross, I suppose." He still didn't look at her.

"All right. Do you own a suit? It would be nice if you could wear a suit."

Lawrence squirmed in the chair. "Yes Ma'am. I have a suit, but it's pretty old and worn out."

"Well, it will have to do." Miss Uremovich stood and looked down at her husband-to-be. "Where shall we live?" When Lawrence remained dumb, she continued, "I guess we can live here in the teacherage. If you work for Anson Gross you can ride from here each morning in time to be there for breakfast. "

Lawrence finally stirred, looked up at her and said,

"Ma'am, I ain't never thought about marriage before."

"I asked you to call me Myrtle. Please do so from now on." She reached down, took his hand to ease him to his feet. "We must get acquainted. You may come here to visit with me Monday for one hour in the evening. I'll expect you at seven o'clock. Then we'll decide about further visits." She led him to the door. "You seem to be a nice man. I'm sure we'll get along."

Ruby couldn't keep the joke to herself so she told Chastity. "Those dumb men think they played a joke on the teacher. But she's smarter than they are. She's going let 'em think she'll marry that boy. And then at the last minute she'll call it off."

Chastity cackled her coarse laugh at the idea and promised to help in any way that she could. She suggested they plan a reception at the saloon and offered to provide the refreshments. Her conniving mind told her there would be a need for lots of whiskey, once the charade was exposed.

****

Lawrence told Anton Gross what had happened, all the while looking down at the ground.

Anton shook his head and said, "Lawrence, you'd been drinking and can't be responsible for your actions when you were drunk. You should tell the teacher now, before this thing goes any farther."

"No sir, I asked her, and she said yes. It was wrong, and I knew it was wrong when I did it. I ain't going to embarrass her any more. I'll go through with it." Finally he looked up at his employer and asked, "Can I stay at the teacherage at night, as long as I get here in time to work in the morning?"

"Hell, yes, Lawrence, but you'd better think this thing through. It's your whole life you're talking about.

The young man heaved a sigh. "Yes, sir. I know. "

****

The wedding day arrived, warm and clear. Ruby and Chastity could hardly contain themselves as they waited for the ceremony to begin. Miss Uremovich had given no indication of the point at which she intended to put a stop to the foolishness. They finally decided she would do it just before the preacher started to read from his book.

The hotel lobby was packed with as many people as its small size would allow. All the miscreants who had started the whole fiasco were in attendance, still snickering at the brilliance of their idea. The groom waited near the registration desk with Anton by his side. His suit was two sizes too small and had a patch on the elbow of the coat. The bride entered through the door leading from the living quarters. The dress she wore differed not a whit from the ones she wore each day to teach. Ruby, standing beside Mss Uremovich, glanced over her shoulder at Chastity and winked.

The preacher began his incantation. "We are gathered here…" Lawrence coughed and looked at his bride for the first time since she came in the room. She smiled at him during that brief moment. Then his gaze returned to the floor.

Ruby saw the smile and thought, "Here it comes. She's about to call it off and laugh at the whole bunch."

The preacher went on reading from his black book—and nobody stopped him. When it was obvious that he was about to speak the fatal words, "I now pronounce you man and wife," Ruby felt ill. Miss Uremovich wasn't going to stop ceremony. She was going to become Mrs. McManus. Why, Ruby wondered, would she do that? Marry a simple-minded cowpuncher?

The preacher ended his spiel with the traditional words, "You may now kiss the bride." Lawrence was sweating. The new Mrs. McManus turned her face to him, showing her homely smile, and he did the required thing. He pecked her quickly on the lips.

The crowd, including Ruby and Chastity, broke into cheers and clapping. Stage Stop had a newly married couple.

****

It's hell to be confined to this chair. Being old ain't no fun. But life has been damn good. Bobby runs this ranch better than I ever did. And it was nice of him to name his boy Larry, after me. Of course, I was named after my grandfather, Lawrence McManus. He must have been a helluva man. Put this outfit together from scratch and then left it to Pa, and Pa left it to me. Thirty thousand acres and a thousand cows. I guess his wife, Grandma Myrtle, had a lot to do with it.

They were old, of course, when I was a child, but I still remember what they looked like. She was taller, probably because one of his legs bowed way out to the side. They said a horse fell on him once, and it never healed straight. She always wore a black dress. He never wore anything but his work clothes. The nice thing was, they were always holding hands. They sure seemed to love each other.

I've always wondered how they met.

SWAMP

Swamp sat with his back against the side of the shack and watched as Flower struggled to mend a pair of his breeches. There was no other hide available so she'd cut a small piece from the remnants of a teepee to make a patch. There was no sinew for stitching, nor was she able to get any thread from the agency so she was trying to use hawthorns as fasteners to hold the patch in place. He was sure the time spent would be wasted. She never ceased in her effort to preserve some semblance of the life they had once known. Her ingenuity had been often tested, as it was at the moment. Still she persisted.

Only four summers ago, he had been hunting for buffalo. Only four summers ago, there were hides for clothing and meat for food. Only four summers ago, he had never seen a white man. Now he spent each day just sitting and waiting for time to pass. There were few buffalo left. No one was allowed off the reservation to hunt, even if they could find buffalo to kill. He was helpless to provide for her and for himself. There was nothing to indicate it would ever change.

The white men said to learn their ways, to forget the days when they lived as hunters. "Swamp, stay in one place," they said. "Swamp, build a house that is permanent." "Swamp, learn to farm," they said. He didn't know why the white men called him Swamp. It wasn't his name. But they made all of the decisions now. They even decided what names he and his people should have.

He wanted to get along with them, because there didn't seem to be anything else to do. So he dug dirt out of the hillside and then used some logs and boards that he had scavenged to build the shack. But it was a miserable hovel. Nothing like a teepee. It was dark and gloomy during the summer. In the winter it was cold, dank and smoky. When it rained, as it had the past few days, the water poured down through the slab board and sod roof.

He tried to learn to farm. But the agent provided few of the tools and equipment that were promised. That promise, like all of the others, was worthless. So he and the others were dependent on the handouts from the agency. They were supposed to get beef on a regular basis. But the animals given to them were, at best, emaciated and, at worst, diseased and near death. And there were never enough animals to feed all the people who were confined to the reservation.

Swamp looked again at the woman as she struggled with her task. He called her Flower. She reminded him of the loveliness of growing things. Twenty years ago, when she came to live in his teepee, she had been shapely and pretty to look at. Now she was only bones. The lack of food was wasting her away. And he wasn't any better.

They were slowly dying because they didn't have enough to eat.

He pulled his cloak around his shoulders. After the rain, a cold wind had started to blow from the east. Even though it was summer, they both needed all of their clothing to keep warm. Under the cloak was the pistol—with two bullets in it.

As was often the case of late, he wondered how it all could have happened—and in such a short time. Only four summers ago, his people had wiped out the soldiers on the stream the white men called the Little Big Horn. And before that, they had defeated a huge army of soldiers on the river they called the Rosebud. His people thought the white men had learned a lesson and would leave them alone. That's all that he and his people wanted—just to be left alone.

Swamp had taken the pistol from one of the dead soldiers at the Little Big Horn. The agent and the soldiers didn't know he had it.

After Little Big Horn, spirits were high. The tribes had gone on the summer hunt thinking that the buffalo range would be theirs forever. But the white men followed and harassed them constantly. When winter came they were never at peace. Always, there were soldiers hunting for red men. When they found an Indian camp they attacked it mercilessly with no regard for women and children. So Swamp and his band moved their camp constantly to try to avoid discovery. And they fought when they were attacked. Many of them died, either from the winter cold or in running fights with the soldiers.

The white men kept sending word that they should go to the reservation. The white men promised that there would be plenty of cattle for them to butcher and other food for them to eat. The white men would provide it all. The white men promised that life for the red men would be good. And the white men promised that there would be no more fighting.

So finally they went to the reservation. But life was not the way they had been told it would be. There was never enough food of any kind, and the agent dictated every aspect of their lives. They were prisoners without walls.

He and others of his band tried to live as they were told. But finally they could not bear to watch their women and children starve. Last summer they left the reservation to hunt. They soon found that the white men had destroyed nearly all of the buffalo. The white men had killed them, not to use the meat, but just to take the hides. Swamp and his little band finally located a small herd of the great beasts and killed four of them. They were skinning and dressing the carcasses when the soldiers came. The soldiers ordered them to leave their kill and return to the reservation immediately. Swamp asked that they be allowed to complete their task and take the meat and hides with them. The officer in charge became angry and told them they would be shot if they didn't move immediately. Little Wolf became angry too. He started toward the officer, waving his skinning knife and shouting that they needed the meat to stay alive. Before he traveled four steps, some of the soldiers began beating him with the butts of their rifles. He fell to the ground, but they did not stop beating on him until he was unconscious. When his woman ran to try to protect him, the officer pulled his handgun and shot her in the head. She fell to the ground, dead.

Swamp remembered it again and felt sick. Neither he nor any of the others could do anything about the atrocity. The soldiers were well fed and they had the rifles. He and the others were helpless.

The officer then yelled at the rest of the band to start for the reservation immediately or he would have his soldiers start shooting. They moved to take the dead woman with them but the soldiers wouldn't allow it. They tried to help the beaten man, but the soldiers drove them away. They looked back, as they straggled toward the far off reservation, to see the soldiers loading the helpless man on a horse, like a sack of grain. The dead woman was still lying on the grass.

Five days later, they hanged Little Wolf. Everyone on the reservation was required to watch. Two soldiers dragged him from the place where they had him locked up. Because of the beating, he still couldn't walk. While he was lying on the ground by the gallows, they tied his hands behind him. Two soldiers had to hold him erect so they could put the rope around his neck. It took him a long time to die. Once again, Swamp and the others were helpless.

He looked at Flower when they did it to Little Wolf. She had her hands over her eyes and was weeping. She must think him a coward. And she must know that he could no longer protect her and their daughter.

They were graced with two children. Their son died of the pox that the white men brought. Their daughter had grown to be a handsome girl of fifteen summers. Then, two moons ago, a white trapper walked up to the child when they were at the agency. He grabbed her by the arm, and growled, "Come on. You're mine now."

Swamp's anger overcame any fear, and he doubled his fists and started to run at the trapper. But his daughter raised her hand to stop him. "At least he'll be able to get food for me." There was a look of resignation on her face when she said it. Then she followed the filthy man out of their lives.

Thinking of it again, Swamp fingered the gun under his cloak. He used it once to shoot an antelope when the agency people couldn't see him. It took all but two of the bullets to kill the animal because it was far away and difficult to hit. He might have used the two remaining bullets when they went to hunt the buffalo, but he now was glad that he hadn't done so.

The boys of his clan still pretended that the old ways would return. They got together in small groups and bragged to each other about how they would kill the soldiers and hunt the buffalo again. And they bragged to each other about their horses and what fine animals each of them had. Swamp had seen the horses. They were a pitiful lot, not suited for either fighting or hunting.

Once Swamp had several fine horses. The soldiers took all of them but one. Not long ago, a young man from the tribe came to Swamp's hovel and demanded the horse. Swamp refused him, but the youth had taken the horse anyway. Swamp was too weak to fight someone so young, someone who still had strength. As the young man walked away, he sneered back over his shoulder at Swamp, "What are you going to do? Tell the agent?"

It would do no good to tell the agent. The agent would just tell Swamp that his people were supposed to settle their own quarrels. So now he had no horses at all.

Flower muttered in frustration and threw the breeches aside. There were tears in her eyes. He was certain that she felt as helpless as he did. They were living a life without hope.

He fingered the pistol again.

How nice it would be to go away from the reservation, to a place where they could live as they had when they were young. He looked at the woman who had shared his life, the one who had suffered all of the tragedies with him. The decision was easy to make.

He stood and went to her with a smile and with his hand outstretched. "Come. Let us go over beyond the trees. It's time that we found a place to rest."

She hesitated only a moment and then got to her feet. The look in her eyes told him that she understood.

They walked, hand in hand, away from the desolate shack and the worn out breeches to the place where they would once again find peace. Beyond the trees they would sit together, and then they would leave forever that hellish place that white men called a reservation.

BARS' REPUTATION

"They're headed south on the run. The tracks are plain enough." There was a long pause while the boss looked toward the Two Dot Butte. "I expect they'll stop before long and start to graze. You should find 'em without any trouble." The old man looked off toward the Butte once again with his hands on his hips, then back at Grove. Finally he mumbled to himself, "Must have been the damn elk that tore the fence down. I thought the nesters had killed 'em all."

The boy grabbed the stirrup and climbed into the saddle. "Don't worry. I'll bring 'em back."

Grove kicked his pony into a slow trot and headed in the direction the loose horses had taken. When he looked back, his father was stepping up into the buggy to return to the ranch buildings. Once the old man was out of sight, Grove slowed his mount to a walk. The boss was correct. The horses wouldn't go far before they tired of the run. Then they'd settle down to graze. And when the day got hot, the horses would find a hilltop where they would stand and fight flies. That's when Grove expected to find them.

At eight o'clock in the morning the day was still

pleasantly cool, and Grove was glad that he didn't have to waste it riding on a dump rake. Instead, he could enjoy a leisurely horseback ride while everyone else sweated, putting up hay.

The tracks led him south, around the lower part of the Two Dot Butte. He followed them up the small creek between that butte and the Coffin Butte. The horses were still on the run—much to Grove's surprise—as evident from the tracks that were plain to see. The trail wound along over the top of the divide and continued on down into the basin beyond. He'd traveled more than seven miles and wondered why the horses hadn't slowed their pace. By now, they'd be far ahead of him. He should have been moving faster.

When Grove reached the floor of the basin, the air was getting hot. He slipped off his jacket and tied it behind his saddle. Then he kicked his horse into a trot as he continued to follow the tracks toward the foot of the Crazy Mountains. Shortly, however, the trail disappeared onto the long shale flat that stretched away on the south side of the Coffin Butte. Grove rode on toward the south, expecting to pick up the tracks again. No luck.

With a shake of his head, he began a great circle around the general area where the tracks should have reappeared beyond the shale, but didn't find any sign of them. Finally, the young man stopped at a spring, dismounted while his horse drank the cold water, and lifted his hat to scratch his head as he thought. He didn't dare return to the ranch without the lost horses. His father, who was "the boss" to him and to everyone else on the ranch, would never understand how he could lose the trail. Grove threw his hat on the ground, gave it a kick, and then gathered up some of the spring water in his hands and scrubbed his face to cool down. That done, he said to himself, "Well, they were headed for the mountains, and they're probably still going in that direction." Jamming his hat on his head, he climbed back on his horse and started off again at a trot.

Grove hit the timberline near Little Elk Creek and then followed the timber around the foot of Loco Mountain toward the south. Whenever he reached a high place, he spent time scanning the country that sloped away in the distance. But the lost animals were nowhere to be seen. Midday came and went. His belly reminded him that it had been a long time since the morning meal. At seventeen years of age, he had a healthy appetite and wished he'd eaten more hotcakes at breakfast. He also wished he'd carried a can of tomatoes wrapped in his slicker and then tied behind the cantle of his saddle. Cold canned tomatoes were good to eat on a hot afternoon.

It was late in the day when the youngster rode over a small rise to see a cabin snuggled in a grove of trees in the bottom of a draw. Until that moment he'd been wondering if he should give up and start home or sleep out and continue his search in the morning. The cabin offered an alternative. If it was empty, he could in move for the night. If it was occupied, the occupant would undoubtedly invite him to stay. Grove stopped his horse near a hitch rail. He walked to the door and was about to knock when he heard a sound around the side of the cabin to his left. He turned to walk in that direction and then felt a sharp jab in his back. A deep voice growled, "Don't move."

Grove jerked from the pain and turned his head to look behind only to be jabbed again, this time even harder. The voice came louder and sounded meaner. "I said, don't move."

The young man's hungry belly turned to ice, and he started to raise his hands to the sky. This time the jab was fierce. "You don't listen, do you? Dammit, I said don't move." Grove froze in place.

It seemed a long time before the man moved around so that Grove, peering out of the corner of his eye, could get a look at him. He was huge, ugly, and angry. "What the hell are you doin'? Tryin' to sneak up on old Bars?" The rifle in his hands remained pointed at Grove's midsection. It was a 45-90-caliber saddle gun. The hole in the muzzle looked the size of the one in the snout of a cannon.

"I wasn't sneaking up on anybody. I rode in here wide open and started to knock on the door. What's the matter with you, anyway?"

"Smart young pup, ain't you." The look of anger faded away and the voice turned kindly. "Well, you look harmless enough. Come on in. I'm about to cook supper." The unkempt creature propped the rifle against the door jamb and led the way into the cabin. Grove felt a moment of relief and then came anger. His back hurt, and he had been scared worse than ever before in his life. The thought of supper overcame the anger, though, and he followed the old reprobate through the door.

Because the man with the rifle was dressed in filthy clothes, Grove expected the cabin to be filthy, too. Much to his surprise, the interior was neat and spotlessly clean. His host—if that's what the man was—stoked the fire in the stove and then scrubbed his hands in a wash basin carefully, using lots of soap. He directed Grove to sit in a chair at the small table, while he fried up some meat and potatoes. He produced a can of the tomatoes, the food that had been so much on Grove's mind. All the while he whistled a tuneless melody through his teeth and said not a word to his guest.

The cook scattered a couple of tin plates and some worn knives and forks on the table. He poured water into two chipped cups and placed the food, still in the pans in which it had been cooked, between the plates. The tomatoes were left in the open can. Some stale bread chunks in a small saucer completed the offering. When all was arranged, the old man pulled up a chair and said, "Eat."

Grove was hungry, as hungry as he had ever been, so he piled food on his plate and dug in. He made no attempt at conversation. He just ate. As he began to fill up, however, the pace of his eating slowed. That gave him an opportunity to size up the man across the table. He saw features that were coarse and skin that was so burned by the sun as to be nearly black. There was a huge bruise below the left eye. The face was deeply wrinkled like that of a man seventy years of age. Except for those wrinkles, he appeared to be about fifty years old. The hands working the eating utensils were huge, and the knuckles were like the knots on a knurled cedar. Grove gulped at a mouthful of spuds when it dawned on him who he had stumbled onto. That stopped his chewing for a moment. But hunger immediately started him up again.

Grove's dining companion did his share with the grub, and it was soon gone. The youngster leaned back in his chair and, without thinking, patted his stomach. The older man scooted his chair around and stretched out his legs as he picked at his teeth with the nail on his little finger. "They call me Bars. What's your name?"

"I'm Grove—Grover. My mother named me after the president."

"Well, Cleveland wasn't so bad. Not as bad as old Teddy Roosevelt that we're stuck with now, anyway. What's your last name?"

"Linton. My father is John Linton. And he's spoken of you. You must be Bars Brown. I think my Pa said your name was Barsness Brown."

"Yup. You've got me right. I guess my mother didn't

like me neither, to give me a name like that. I never saw her so I don't know." He squinted across the table at Grove. "And, I'll be damned. So you're old Linton's son." Bars scratched his armpit. "But what're you doin' clear over here?"

"Some horses ran off, and my father sent me to find 'em. So far I haven't had any luck."

Bars swiveled around in his chair so that he was looking straight at Grove. His face took on a crafty appearance. "What's your Pap told you about me?"

Grove's eyebrows went up. "What has Pa told me about you?" He hesitated for a moment and squirmed a little in his chair. "Well, for one thing, he says you're the toughest man in the valley. I guess you've whipped 'em all."

That remark drew a hoarse laugh. "I damn near got whupped last Saturday in Melville. Young George Hammerness decided to try me. He might of got it done, too, 'cause he was pretty fast with his fists. And, damn, he could hit hard." Bars touched the bruise on his face gently with one finger. "But he was wearing wooly chaps and couldn't move around very good. When I got him on the floor, where I could really pound on him, he pretty quick squawked that he'd had enough."

Grove looked at the huge, lumpy fists and thought how painful it would be to have those hammering on his face.

Bars scratched at his armpit some more before he

asked the next question. "What else did your Pap tell you? Didn't he tell you that I'm a cattle rustler? A horse thief? Someone who ought to be in the state pen?"

Grove was reluctant to answer that question. He'd never heard his father accuse Bars of being a thief, but when Bars name was mentioned there was invariably someone in the group who would make that accusation. Bars spoke again, so Grove didn't have to answer.

"It don't make no difference. We all have a reputation and have to live up to it. Your Pap has a reputation too." Grove raised his eyebrows again and wondered what would come next. "He has a reputation for honesty. They say that John Linton never took even a penny that didn't belong to him." The wrinkles formed into a grin. "Now that's a reputation! And it's probably true." The grin got wider. "What do you think?"

"Of course Pa's honest. Why wouldn't he be?"

"That's it. He don't have to steal. He's got his ranch and everything he needs, including a son. I suppose it's easy to be honest when you've got it all."

Grove started to ask Bars if he was dishonest because he needed to be, but thought better of it. Instead he turned the conversation back to the lost horses. "You know the country around here. Where could those horses have gone?" When Bars didn't respond, he added, "If you'll let me stay the night, I'll start after 'em again in the morning."

"Of course, you stay the night. What did you think

I'd do? Feed you and then throw you out?" He got up from the table and started to gather the dishes to wash them. "We'll talk about the horses in the morning."

****

Bars shoved the breakfast dishes out of the way and drank the last swallow of coffee before he rose from his chair. "You ain't goin' to find them horses by just wandering around the countryside. I'll tell you what. You go on back home. I know this country. The horses'll show up around here somewhere. When they do, I'll let you know, and you can come and get 'em."

Grove thought for a minute and decided the old man was right. He had no idea where to go next to try to locate the lost animals. He may as well get back to the ranch and report to his father. Bars would likely find the horses and send word. His father would understand. So he thanked his host for the grub and bed, turned his horse north, and started the long ride home.

"You did what?" The Boss's voice was loud and incredulous. "You told Bars Brown that we'd lost some horses? And that they were headed his way?" He stalked around the room as he talked. "Well, that'll be the end of that bunch. He'll find the horses, all right, and have 'em out of the country before we can do anything about it."

"But he said that he'd let us know if he found them."

"Son, Bars Brown isn't going to report anything to us except maybe that he didn't find 'em. Those horses are easy money for him. He knows how to move 'em out of the country without anyone knowing it. And he has people who will pay him for 'em, then re-brand 'em, and sell 'em somewhere a long way from here. Those horses are gone for good." The Boss started for the door. "Well, I'll go to Two Dot tomorrow and send a telegram to the sheriff in White Sulphur Springs—for whatever good that will do."

****

Grove spent the next two days wondering if he should sneak away and go back to Bars' camp. He might find the horses somewhere between here and there. Or, if Bars had the horses, he might persuade the man to return them to the owner. He didn't mention the possibility to his father. If the Boss thought such a trip would do any good, he would have already sent Grove on his way. Instead of running off on a hopeless mission, he just went ahead with the daily tasks that were assigned to him.

The third day after his return from the horse hunt, Grove was sent to dig post holes around a haystack that was tucked behind some thick brush along the creek. He'd finished his task and was hitching the team to the wagon when he caught the pain of a rifle prodding him in the back once again. This time he knew what was happening and had a good idea who was doing the prodding. He turned to find Bars standing there, rifle in hand, grinning at him.

"Well, at least you didn't jump out of your hide like

you almost did the last I snuck up on you." Bars put the rifle butt down on the ground and leaned on the barrel while he waited for Grove's reaction.

"Someday, someone is going to shoot you for doing that. It isn't funny."

"Before anyone can shoot me, they've got to get the drop on me. And no one's done it yet." He chuckled. "Beside, who'd want to shoot old Bars. I'm easy to get along with." The chuckle turned to laughter. "But poking a rifle in your back isn't the reason I'm here." He turned and started toward a small opening in the brush, then looked back at Grove. "I've found your horses. The Mexican had 'em at his camp near the head of Sweetgrass Creek. It ain't no wonder that you couldn't catch up with 'em. He ran 'em all the way to his place from where he tore your fence down." Bars was talking as he walked. "The Mex was just about to start to Miles City with 'em when I got there. After I got done with him, he was glad to let me lead 'em away." Bars jerked his head at Grove. "Come on. I got 'em tied next to the creek, out of sight."

Just as Bars said, all of the lost animals were hitched in a long line to a downed cottonwood tree. The two men led them out and tied the horses head to tail so that Grove could lead them home behind the wagon. When they were ready to go and before Grove could say a word, Bars climbed onto his saddle horse. He turned to Grove one more time. "Them halters belong to the Mexican. I expect your Pap to pay the Mex for 'em—even if that devil did intend to steal his prize stock. After all, each of us has a reputation to protect. And your old man wouldn't want to ruin the one he has by making off with another man's halters." He was laughing as he headed off toward the mountains.

Grove stood for a long time, watching him ride away. Finally he yelled as loud as he could, "Well, you've sure as hell ruined your reputation as a horse thief."

Bars just laughed louder and never looked back.

HARRY'S RIDE TO KNOTHOLE

SATURDAY

The storekeeper left the telephone receiver dangling by its cord and walked to the back of the store where the sheriff was picking through a pile of shirts on the counter. "Percy Esp wants to talk to you. He said Harry's quit again. That cowpuncher's on his best horse, and he's headed for town."

The sheriff, tall and stout, nodded his head and said, "I'm not surprised. It's been six months." At the front of the store and with the telephone to his ear, he leaned into the mouthpiece. "Percy? This is Alex. How much money does Harry have?"

Percy's voice was faint coming over the one wire telephone line that served the eleven ranches strung out along Skunk Creek. "He had six months pay coming, so I gave him a check for three hundred dollars."

"That's fifty a month. I thought the going wage was thirty."

"It is. But Harry's the best cowman and the best horse hand in this valley. He's better than any three other cowdogs I could hire. I pay him what he's worth."

"That seems fair." The sheriff was silent for a moment, then asked, "Did you give him the lecture?"

"I sure as hell did. Just like before. I told him that whiskey was going to be his ruination." It was Percy's turn to pause. "And just like before, he'll ignore it."

The sheriff coughed to the side and then said, "Well, thanks for the call. I'll let the barkeepers and the others know that Harry's on his way." The sheriff placed the receiver on its hook on the side of the wall telephone and tromped out the door and down the street toward the courthouse in Knothole, county seat of Grassland County. He was headed for the office of the county attorney.

That worthy gentleman, old and small, leaned back in his chair while looking up at the sheriff standing in front of the desk. "How long do you think it'll take him to get the job done?"

"Four days should do it." The sheriff pushed his hat to one side as he scratched his head. "We'll need paint, a brush, and some turpentine."

"How much will it cost?"

"Twenty-five dollars should cover it all."

"All right. I'll tell the justice of the peace. You be sure to tell Jeff at the Stockman how much money we need."

"I'll do it." The sheriff straightened his hat and turned to leave. Over his shoulder he added, "Last time Jeff forgot—or said he did. I'll make sure that doesn't happen again."

WEDNESDAY

The justice of the peace, a retired carpenter who was stooped and scrawny, didn't have a courtroom. Now, three days after Harry rode into town, the justice was holding court in the back room of the general store. "Harry, you're charged with being drunk and disorderly. How do you plead?"

At other times, Harry was a handsome young man—six feet of hard muscle when he stood straight. But right now, he was leaning on the back of a chair, grasping it tightly with both hands to keep from falling down. His face was pasty white. His eyes were bleary and failed to focus. His hair was mussed and filthy. Since he'd arrived in town, he'd acquired a suit of clothes of a greenish color. One leg of the pants was torn at the knee. The buttons were ripped from the front of the coat. Harry had lost his dinner the night before, and the once white shirt was stained down the front.

When Harry didn't answer, the justice asked again, "How do you plead?"

The miscreant shook his head as though to clear his mind and looked around at the sheriff on one side, the county attorney on the other, and finally at the justice in front of him. "Where am I?"

The sheriff grabbed his arm to straighten him up and

said, "You're in court, Harry. You've raised hell the past three days, busted the window out of the Stockman Bar, punched the barkeep at the Mint, and smashed his nose. And you scared poor old Mrs. Brown almost to death by trying to kiss her."

Harry shook his head again and turned his bleary eyes toward the peace officer. "God, Sheriff, I didn't do that, did I?"

"Do what?"

"Try to kiss Mrs. Brown?"

"You sure did. And she's mad as hell about it."

Harry pulled the chair around and sat down. His head dropped forward as he looked down at the pointed shoes on his feet. "God, my feet hurt. Where're my boots?"

"They're in my office with your regular clothes." The sheriff pulled on Harry's arm in an attempt to get him on his feet again, but the rapscallion just dropped his hands down between his legs and moaned.

The county attorney cleared his throat and interjected himself into the proceedings. "He pleads guilty, judge. Just like he always does." Turning to the man in the chair, he asked, "That's right, isn't it?"

Harry moaned again and mumbled, "If you say so."

"All right, Judge. Sentence him."

The justice of the peace nodded his head a couple of times in what appeared to be an attempt to get his thoughts going. Then he announced with solemn dignity,

"Harry Hanratty, I sentence you to five days in the county jail, and I fine you the sum of twenty-five dollars." He took a breath and then continued, "While you're in jail, you're going to paint it. If you get done sooner than five days, the sheriff is directed to let you out."

Harry looked at the sheriff out of the corner of his eye and asked, "Can I just sleep for a while before I start to paint?" He rubbed his hand through his rumpled hair. "And can I get my regular clothes?" Dropping his eyes to his feet, he said, "These shoes are killing me. I need my boots."

The sheriff pulled him out of the chair and said, "You've slept for most of a day in the jail. I figure you need at least another day to get plumb sober before you start painting. I'll bring a tub of water to the jail this afternoon so you can clean up. And then you'll get your regular clothes back."

Harry started searching through the pockets of the suit, one at a time. At last he shook his head some more and grunted, "I don't have twenty-five dollars."

"Never mind. Jeff at the Stockman Bar took it out of the money you were throwing around. You blew the rest of it on booze and that damned suit. Jeff brought the twenty-five to me yesterday, so the fine is paid."

"Did you give it to the judge?"

"Hell no! How do you think we bought the paint?" Harry shook his head again as though in sorrow at the folly of his ways. As he stumbled to the door, the cowpuncher stopped and looked back at the justice of the peace. "Didn't I paint the jail the last time I got drunk?"

"No. That was three times ago. The last time you painted the hallway in the school."

MONDAY

The sheriff walked into the county attorney's office four days later. Short and rotund Percy Esp trailed behind him. Each man pulled a chair away from in front of the desk, put his hat on the floor, and sat with his feet stretched out comfortably before him. The lawyer directed his question at Percy. "So Harry's back at the ranch?"

"Yup. He rode in this morning."

The sheriff leaned back and said, "Harry finished painting the jail right after he had breakfast. Then he scooted out of town as fast as that old pony would go."

Percy chimed in. "When he got to the ranch he was sober and sorry. And he wondered if I'd take him back. Thought he might have quit one time too many." Percy grinned. "This time I made him beg." The rancher leaned forward in the chair. "And I told him he was throwing his life away on booze. Told him if he kept it up he'd be working for me for the rest of his life and never get a place of his own."

The county attorney turned to the sheriff. "When you turned him loose, did you give him the lecture?"

"Just like I always do, only this time I was more

forceful. I made it plain that responsible men don't touch likker—ever—under any circumstance."

"And his reaction?"

"Same as always. He said he'd never drink again."

"And what did he say to you, Percy?"

"Same thing he told the sheriff."

The lawyer scooted around in his chair. "Well, in six months, Harry'll quit again. Ain't that right, Percy?"

"Right."

The attorney shuffled around in the documents on his desk and pulled a piece of paper from the pile. "This is a letter from the district judge. He says the next time that man gets drunk we're to have him paint the courtroom."

The sheriff mused, "I was thinking the outside of the school needs paint. But I guess we shouldn't argue with the judge."

"No, we shouldn't." The county attorney leaned down and pulled a bottle of rye whiskey and three glasses from a desk drawer. He carefully placed the glasses on the desktop and poured a generous measure of the liquid into each of them. He shoved one glass toward the sheriff, one toward Percy Esp, and picked up one for himself. For a moment he looked across the desk at his companions and then offered, "Here's to Harry Hanratty. May he never take the temperance pledge."

Raising their glasses, the sheriff and the rancher responded in unison, "I'll drink to that!"

THE TESTIMONY OF TOBY WORTH

"The State calls Toby Worth."

Tom Wilkerson, County Attorney of Grassland County, turned to look over his shoulder at the small boy seated between his parents in the front row of the audience section. The boy leaned forward, paused, then put his hands on the bench to push himself to a standing position. He took a deep breath, looking first at his father and then at his mother. His father shifted, as if to stand with him, but instead, simply reached out to pat his son on the shoulder. The child smiled a wan smile at his parents and turned to face the front of the courtroom. His father slumped down on the bench with his arm around his wife. She nervously clutched a handkerchief that was damp with perspiration.

The diminutive witness walked slowly through the little gate that led to the area before the judge's bench, as he had seen other witnesses do, and then stopped in front of the clerk of court and held up his hand. The clerk recited the oath that required the witness to tell the truth. Toby Worth dutifully responded, "I do." He hesitated and gave a quick glance upward at the fearsome looking man in the black robe who was seated behind the large, dark colored desk. The judge merely gestured impatiently toward the witness chair.

The boy had to jump to get into the chair and, once there, he found that his feet didn't touch the floor. Before he was fully settled the judge asked, "Do you understand the meaning of the oath you just took?"

The judge's bushy eyebrows were pulled together in a perpetual scowl, and Toby knew from listening to the prior proceedings that explosive anger seemed to erupt from the man without real provocation. He bobbed his head and answered, "Yes sir, I do. It means I have to tell the truth." He inhaled sharply and said, "Yes, Your Honor." He blinked at the judge and added, "My dad says I'm to call you Your Honor. Is that right?"

"That's right. And don't you forget it." Still scowling, the judge added, "The charge is homicide. Do you know what that means?"

"Yes, Your Honor. It means someone got killed."

The judge nodded once, turned to the county attorney and said, "You may proceed, Mr. Wilkerson."

The attorney, standing by the podium, said, "Mr. Worth, please state your full name for the court record."

"My name is Toby Hamilton Worth."

"How old were you on August eighteenth of last year, Toby?"

When Wilkerson saw the defense attorney begin to rise to his feet. He quickly added, "That year would have been 1952."

Toby asked, "Was that the day of the fire?"

"Yes, it was."

"I was nine then. I'm ten now. My birthday was just a month ago."

The attorney said, "Is it all right if I call you Toby ?"

After the boy nodded his consent, he asked, "What were you doing on August eighteenth last year?"

Toby's attention had shifted for a moment to Mrs. Keeler, seated amongst the other jurors in the front row of the jury box. The smile on her face reminded him how nice she was as his fourth grade teacher. Then he remembered where he was, and his head jerked around in response to the question. "Do you mean from the time I got up until I went to bed?"

"No. We just want to know about the things that happened after your father asked you to look at some cattle."

Oliver Arthur, the defense attorney, jumped to his feet to say, "Objection! There's no evidence before the court that this boy's father asked him to do anything."

The judge's scowl deepened, and he spoke with evident impatience. "Mr. Arthur, the witness is very young, and Mr. Wilkerson is trying to set the stage for his testimony. Your objection is overruled." Turning to Toby, he said, "You may answer the question if you remember what it is."

"Yes, sir. I mean Your Honor. I think I know what

the question is." Toby looked at the county attorney and started swinging his feet above the floor as he spoke. "My dad asked me to take Tanglefoot and ride up the creek to see if the cattle in the Sandy Bluffs pasture were out of salt."

"Who is Tanglefoot?"

Toby's freckles seemed to become three times larger when he smiled. "Tanglefoot's my horse." The boy paused and then added, "Well, he's really kind of a pony. Dad named him Tanglefoot because he stumbles once in while." He smiled at Mrs. Keeler and the other members of the jury and then went on, "So I caught Tanglefoot and saddled him up." He turned to look at the judge as he continued to talk. "I can saddle him 'cause he's pretty small, and Dad got me a saddle that's my size and doesn't weight as much as his." The judge merely nodded, the scowl still in place, and looked toward the county attorney as though impatient for the next question.

"After the horse was saddled, what did you do?"

Toby turned back to face Mr. Wilkerson. "I rode up the creek." When the county attorney didn't say anything, he continued, "It's about two miles to the pasture. When I got there, I rode around to the places where my dad puts the salt to see if it was all gone. It wasn't"

"What time of day was this?"

Toby sat still and looked upward toward the ceiling as he thought. "I left the ranch after breakfast and after I caught and saddled Tanglefoot. And it took a while to get there. Maybe it was ten o'clock when I started home."

"Did you see anything different on your way home than you saw on your way to the pasture?"

"You mean the fire?"

"Did you see a fire?"

"Well, when I rode around the bottom of the big hill in Mr. Ziebarth's pasture, I saw a lot of smoke coming from the south, not far from the fence between his land and ours."

"By Mr. Ziebarth, you mean the man seated over there at the defense table, don't you?"

Toby looked in the direction of the table where the defendant and his counsel were sitting.

"Yes, sir. Mr. Ziebarth is our neighbor."

Mr. Wilkerson glanced down at his notes and then asked, "Were you on land belonging to Mr. Ziebarth when you saw the smoke?"

"Yes sir. You see our ranch kind of wraps around his." Toby held up his right hand with his fingers curved in a half circle to show what he meant. "The trail from our ranch to the Sandy Bluffs pasture goes through his land."

Wilkerson stood beside the podium and rested one hand on it. "What happened after you saw the smoke?"

"Well, I rode around the bottom of the big hill, and pretty soon I could see the flames over toward the mountains."

"What was burning?"

"I couldn't tell at first, but when I got up on a little

hill, I could see it was grass burning."

"What else did you see?"

"I could see Mr. Ziebarth's pickup parked near where the fire had burned."

"Could you see Mr. Ziebarth?"

Toby looked over at the defendant, then turned back toward Mr. Wilkerson. "Not at first because of the smoke, but when the smoke kind of blew away I could see someone swinging something near the edge of the fire." He paused and then added, "I thought it must be Mr. Ziebarth 'cause it was his pickup parked out there."

"How big was the fire?"

"It was huge." Toby thought for a moment, looking off into the distance. "Well, the flames weren't so high but the fire was real long. The wind was blowing it to the east, and it was shaped in kind of a half circle." He paused and then corrected himself. "Not a half circle, really, but in a big curve. Kind of like a smile upside down."

"How long was the curve?"

"It was long." The boy stopped again to think before continuing. "It's an eighth of a mile from our house to the mailbox and the fire must have been that long."

"And Mr. Ziebarth was at the end away from you?"

"Yes, sir."

"How close were you to the near end?"

"When I first saw the fire I was quite a ways away. But I rode toward it and was right close when Mr. Ziebarth came up in his pickup."

"You mean he came to where you were?"

"Yes, sir. He drove across the part behind the fire that was burned." Toby looked toward the defendant for a heartbeat, then back at the county attorney. "The fire had burned a long ways. The burned grass went clear over the top of a hill. I heard it started from Mr. Ziebarth's trash barrel."

The defense attorney was on his feet. "Objection, Your Honor, hearsay."

The judge's impatience surfaced again. "Mr. Arthur, there has already been testimony that the fire started as the boy said. Objection overruled."

The county attorney asked, "What did Mr. Ziebarth do when he got to where you were?"

"As I was getting off of Tanglefoot, he jumped out of his pickup and yelled at me to take the saddle off my horse and use the saddle blanket to fight the fire."

"Did he say anything else?"

"He said the hottest part of the fire was at the other end and that he would go back and fight it there. He told me to start beating on the flames at my end with the saddle blanket. Then he got in his pickup again. Just before he drove away he yelled out the window that we could put the fire out if we worked toward each other as fast as we could."

"What did you do then?"

"I took the saddle off and tied the bridle reins to it so

Tanglefoot wouldn't run off. Then I took the blanket and walked to the edge of the fire." Toby swallowed, glanced sideways at the judge and blurted, "It was real hot, and the smoke made me choke." The judge looked down at the boy out of the corner of his eye and maintained his scowl.

Toby turned back to Mr. Wilkerson when he was asked, "Were you able to fight the fire?"

"Well, I had a hard time figuring out how to use the blanket to put out the flames. Finally I just took it by one corner and swung it over my head and then down on the ground. That way I could knock out flames that were right at my feet."

"What was Mr. Ziebarth doing at that time?"

"I guessed he was fighting the fire at the other end, but I couldn't see him most of the time because of the smoke. Once in a while the wind would blow the smoke away and then I could see him swinging something at the fire, kind of like I was doing with the blanket. But he was able to swing a lot faster than I could."

"How long did you continue swinging the blanket?"

The boy looked down at his toes, then over at his parents, then at the judge again. His face, that had been so sunny, took on a pained expression. When he didn't say anything, the judge growled, "Answer the question."

Toby jerked his head up and said, "The blanket got to be awful heavy. I tried to keep swinging at the fire, but pretty soon my arms were so tired that I couldn't do it. I'd have to stop for a while and rest."

"What happened then?"

"I guess Mr. Ziebarth saw me resting cause he came around the fire again in his pickup and yelled at me to get busy. He seemed awful mad, so I tried as hard as I could to keep swinging the blanket. But my arms hurt so bad that I just had to rest every once in a while."

"Toby, were you and Mr. Ziebarth making any headway in fighting the fire?"

"Yes, sir. I kept beating on the fire on my end and he kept beating on the fire on his end and the fire got shorter between us."

"How much shorter?"

"Well, the grass near the fence between our place and Mr. Ziebarth's place was really eaten down on his side. So when the fire got closer to the fence, the flames weren't as high. I found I could just drag the blanket over the top of them and put them out. My boots got awful hot, though, because to pull the blanket, I had to walk in the fire where it was burning. But I didn't want to get yelled at again, so I kept going." He glanced at the defendant and then went on. "When I looked toward Mr. Ziebarth I could see we were really getting close together."

"How close? As close as from here across the street?'

"The boy thought a second, then turned to the judge and asked, "Can I look out the window, Your Honor?"

"Yes, but be quick."

Toby scooted out of the chair and went to one of

the large windows that overlooked the main street of the small town. In only a moment he was back in the chair and said, "We were closer than that. Maybe we were as close as twice the length of this big room."

The county attorney gave the members of the jury time to look from the front of the room to the back, estimate its size and multiply by two. Then he turned to the judge. "About fifty feet, Your Honor?"

"Close enough."

Returning his attention to Toby, he asked, "Was the fire burning all on Mr. Ziebarth's land at that time?"

"Yes sir. And Mr. Ziebarth's land doesn't have as much grass as our land does." He looked toward his father and then back at the county attorney. "My Dad says that he uses his ranch too hard." The defendant turned an angry stare toward Toby's father, and then he growled something into the ear of his attorney.

"What happened when the fire went through the fence onto your land?"

"Well, the grass was good and tall on our side because my Dad keeps that pasture for winter feed. So the fire got a lot higher and a lot hotter. I could hardly get close enough to swing the blanket at it. And I could see that it was even bigger at the end where Mr. Ziebarth had been. The wind was blowing in that direction."

"What do you mean, where Mr. Ziebarth had been?

"As soon as the fire went through the fence onto our land, Mr. Ziebarth came driving around to me again.

When he stopped where I was standing, he just rolled down the window and said, 'There's a cattle buyer in town. Maybe he'll buy my calves. If you just keep going you can put the fire out." Toby sat for a moment without looking at anyone and then said, "And he just drove off across the field and on down the road."

"You mean he just left you there to fight the fire all alone?"

"I guess so. He was gone."

The county attorney let the jury think about that for a long moment, then asked, "How old were you then?"

"I was nine."

"And how tall were you?"

"Well, Mom measures me on my birthday and I was four feet eight inches last month."

"And you were left there all alone to swing the blanket and fight the fire?"

The defense attorney jumped to his feet to shout, "Objection! Asked and answered."

The judge stared at him without speaking, then turned to the county attorney to say, "Yes, I think we all get the picture. The objection is sustained."

Mr. Wilkerson merely nodded. Then he directed another question to the witness. "What did you do after Mr. Ziebarth left you?"

"I tried to keep on fighting the fire but the blanket was too heavy to swing any more, and the wind changed and blew the flames in my direction, and it was so hot I couldn't stand to be near it."

"So what did you do?'

Toby started swinging his feet back and forth and looked down at them while he did so. Just as the judge leaned in his direction to tell him to answer the question, he looked up and said, "I started to cry."

The county attorney stood quietly before asking the next question. "What did you do then?"

"I dragged the blanket back to where Tanglefoot was tied. I hated to put the blanket on him because it was awful black from the ashes so I just left it lying on the ground and put the saddle on without it. I was afraid that my dad would be mad at me because he always told me to be careful when saddling a horse so I didn't do anything to hurt the horse's back." The boy looked down at his feet again. "I was still crying. And I got ashes in my eyes when I rubbed them with my dirty hands and that made me cry some more."

After another pause, Mr. Wilkerson asked, "Toby, what did you do then?"

"I kicked Tanglefoot into a gallop and started back home to tell my dad about the fire. I looked back once and could see that the wind had started to blow harder so the fire got bigger and moved faster. It was headed for the old Harrington Place."

"What is the Harrington Place?"

"Dad has a set of corrals there. And there's an old cabin and a shed that Dad stores things in." Toby looked at his father as he went on. "I was afraid the fire would get there and burn everything up before I could get home."

"So you galloped your horse toward home. What happened along the way?"

"There are two gates I had to go through, and they were both open when I left to go to the Sandy Bluffs pasture. But when I got to the first one going back, it was closed. Someone had put the bulls in that pasture and closed both gates. I opened and closed the first one all right, but when I got to the second one I couldn't close it. It was too tight."

"What did you do?"

"Well, I tried as hard as I could to close the gate 'cause I didn't want the bulls to get into the alfalfa, but I just wasn't strong enough." Once more he looked down at his swinging feet. "I cried some more." Toby glanced up at his mother and then quickly down at his toes. "And I used some bad words."

The boy's mother turned to her husband with a fleeting smile, then wiped at her tears with the handkerchief.

Mr. Wilkerson smiled and asked, "Did the bad words help close the gate?"

"No, sir." The small boy glanced at his mother again and then took a deep breath. "So I finally just left the gate lying on the ground and ran Tanglefoot the rest of the way home."

"What did you do when you got there?"

"I hurried to where my dad was working near his

pickup and told him about the fire. He already knew. He and the men were loading the things they needed to fight it. My dad was telling them what to do." His face brightened when he smiled at his father and said, "My dad knows how to do everything."

His father shuffled his feet, wiped at his eye with the back of his hand, and then pulled his wife even closer.

Toby looked over at the jurors and said, "At first I was afraid to tell him I left the gate open, but then I decided I had to. You see, there's a better road to where the fire was burning than the trail I use on horseback, so no one would be going that way to the fire. I didn't want the bulls to get out, and I figured he could send someone to close the gate."

"What did your father say about the gate?"

"He just said, 'We'll get it later.'" Toby looked again at his father, then smiled at the county attorney. "And he wasn't mad." After another pause, he went on, "Then he told me to hurry and put Tanglefoot in the barn so I could go with him in the pickup."

"Did you tell your father about Mr. Ziebarth?"

Toby looked at the defendant before he answered. "I told him while we were driving to the fire. He didn't say much about Mr. Ziebarth leaving me to fight the fire alone, but I could tell by the look on his face that he didn't like it."

Mr. Ziebarth growled once again in his attorney's

ear. Oliver Arthur just shook his head.

County Attorney Wilkerson shuffled his notes and then asked, "Who beside you and your father went to fight the fire?"

"Dad has three men working for him. Two of them came behind us in the other pickup. Larry—the other men call him Lonesome Larry behind his back cause his girlfriend ran off and married some other guy—was putting gas in the truck that had the water tank and the pump. He came along as soon as he was finished." Toby took a deep breath and waited for a moment. When the county attorney didn't ask a question, he continued, "We followed the road around toward the fire and when we drove over a hill we could see the flames in the distance. They were really big, and there was lots of smoke. Instead of being narrow like Mr. Ziebarth and I left it, it was burning in a long line. The wind was pushing the fire fast, and it was getting close to the Harrington Place.

"What happened then?"

"Dad drove up to the end of the fire where I had been trying to put it out. He jumped out and waved the men in the other pickup toward the other end. Then he grabbed a wet gunnysack—one that was filled with other gunnysacks to make it heavier—from the water barrel that was in the back of the pickup and started to beat on the fire like Mr. Ziebarth had done. He told me to drive the pickup away from the fire. So I did." The boy took a deep breath and blew out a small sigh. "The men, except Larry, were at the other end of the fire beating on it with wet sacks." Toby waited for a question. When none was asked, he went on. "And then the wind came up really hard, and the fire just seemed to run away toward the Harrington Place."

"What happened then?"

"Well, Larry came driving up in the water truck. I guess he could see the fire going toward the buildings because he drove the truck right up close to the storage shed." Toby's eyes widened as he remembered it. "When my dad saw where Larry stopped the truck, he ran toward the shed, yelling as he went. I started after him but he stopped long enough to turn and holler at me to stay away. Then he screamed at Larry to get away from the shed and move the truck." The little boy stopped, sat as still as a statue remembering what had happened. Then he resumed his monologue. "The wind blew a great big gust just before Larry got to the shed, and it carried some burning brush onto the roof. The shingles started to burn and almost right away the whole building seemed to be on fire." Toby looked at his father, who nodded encouragement. "Dad was running and yelling that there was diesel fuel and fertilizer in the shed and it might explode."

"What did Larry do?'

"I guess he couldn't hear Dad…maybe because the water pump on the truck was running. Anyway he just went ahead and pulled the hose out of the truck and turned toward the fire to spray water on it." Toby gulped hard and wiggled in the chair.

The county attorney's face was somber when he said, "Toby, tell us what happened next."

Toby Worth looked down at his toes for a long time before he answered. "Dad was running toward Larry as fast as he could, and Larry was just walking toward the shed with the hose spraying water when all of a sudden there was a huge explosion. It knocked me down." Toby's eyes began to water. "When I sat up I could see my Dad getting up on his feet and staring at the truck." Tears started to run down the cheeks of the small child lost in the large witness chair. "I looked toward the truck, and I could see Larry." Chin trembling, he snuffled and added, "Or what was left of him. He was kind of stuck against the front fender and the radiator of the truck. Most of his clothes were gone and his skin was all black." Toby choked a sob and said, "The fire was so hot." He sobbed some more and finally whimpered very quietly, "And then his skin began to sizzle."

The silence in the courtroom was complete—except for the sobbing of Toby Worth and the sobbing of his mother.

Slowly the child turned to the judge and said, "Your Honor…" Then he gulped and tried again. "Your Honor, I really believe we could have put that fire out if Mr. Ziebarth had only stayed there a little while longer." After that he sat quietly in the big chair, looking at his toes while the tears streamed down his cheeks.

The judge, with a face softened for the first time during the trial, leaned over and patted ten-year-old Toby Worth on the head.

At the same time, Mrs. Keeler, the juror seated in the front row, wrote firmly across the note pad resting on her lap, "GUILTY!"

CUT FENCE

Horace stood looking first at the ruts made by wheels and then at the animal tracks. Someone had driven an automobile through the gap in the fence, and the cattle had followed. A whole bunch of yearlings must have headed west into Shipton's hay field. He pushed his old hat back on his head and swore. Why would anyone cut the fence? The gate at the road wasn't twenty feet away. After he spewed out another string of profanity, the old man kicked at the dirt and turned back to his pickup to get some rusty scraps of wire and fencing pliers. Better to hook the wires back together as best he could right now so that no more of the critters could escape. Proper repairs could be made later.

With the temporary patch in place, Horace hurried to the pickup for a fast drive back to the ranch. He'd get some horses and some help and go after the cattle that strayed. Shipton's second-cutting alfalfa patch was only a mile and a half up the creek.

But why would anyone cut that fence?

The rough road seemed to take an hour. Horace stopped first at the lower meadow where Willis was cutting hay with the swather. He needed the young man to help him hook up the horse trailer and catch a couple of horses. They would haul the horses to the cut fence and then ride west to find the stray animals and bring them home

Willis had worked for Horace for five years, ever since he left school at the age of sixteen. He wasn't overly bright, but he was good with machinery and gentle with livestock. When Horace needed someone to help him with the cattle, he always chose Willis over any of the other ranch hands.

It took a while to get the trailer attached to Horace's ancient four-wheel drive pickup. Then the bald-face gelding wouldn't load until Horace introduced him to a stockyard whip. After the late start and a slow trip back to the fence line, it was nearly six o'clock in the evening before the two men started west on horseback.

Even though the tracks of the cattle appeared to be at least a day old, they were easy to follow where the ground was wet from rain and irrigation. The two men reached the neighbor's alfalfa field and, just as Horace had feared, they found five heifers lying on their sides, legs out stiff, bloated like balloons. The bald-faced horse that Horace was riding was not about to get close enough to the stinking carcasses for Horace to read the brands. Rather than argue with his mount, he got down, handed the reins to Willis, and walked over to take a look. Sure enough, his brand on the left rib of two of the dead cattle was plain to see. Horace stomped back to his horse, all the while cursing the idiot who cut the fence. His voice was almost a screech when he told Willis that he would find that miserable wretch who did it, no matter what it took. When he found him, Horace swore, he would wreak a terrible vengeance.

After venting his wrath, Horace mounted his horse, turned on west and nodded to Willis to follow. The tracks led them through some brush beside the creek to a place where some cattle had bedded down. From there the tracks went north and out onto a shale bench. On the bench, the tracks disappeared. But Horace hadn't spent his life looking after cattle without knowing how they acted. With Willis at his side, he rode farther west and back toward the creek. Soon enough, they topped a small hill and could see the remainder of the heifers grazing in a wild hay meadow, two miles upstream from the alfalfa field.

They gathered the strays and started them back east toward home. Horace ran a count. There were sixteen still alive. Willis followed the animals in silence, but Horace continued his tirade. "Those dead heifers are worth three hundred and fifty dollars apiece when they were alive. That cut fence cost me at least seventeen hundred dollars. Damn, I needed that money, too!" He trotted his horse to push a spooky heifer back with the others. "Well. I'll find out who did it, and by God, he'll pay."

The strays trailed through the gate and back into

their pasture. It was nearly dark, so the men decided to wait till morning to make proper repairs to the fence. While Willis closed the gate, Horace jerked open the back of the horse trailer. When the horses were loaded for the trip home, Horace turned to Willis and asked again, "Why would anybody cut the fence when the gate was so close to it? It just doesn't make any sense."

Willis just mumbled, "I don't know." The young man had learned that when the boss was on a rampage, he didn't want answers to his questions. He didn't even want conversation. He just wanted to spit out his frustrations. Willis maintained his silence the rest of the way to the ranch headquarters.

Horace was calm the next morning when he and Willis drove out to make the fence repairs. They decided they might as well replace a couple of fence posts near the location of the cut wire while they were at it. As they began the work, a car came around the hill from the west. Willis put his shovel down, walked the few steps to the road and opened the gate so Gloria Shipton could drive through. She stopped the car and rolled down the window when Horace headed her way. With her elbow resting on the window ledge, she leaned her head out the window and called out, "Hello, neighbor."

Her greeting made Horace smile. "Good morning, Gloria. Nice day." He took off his hat and wiped his brow on his shirtsleeve. "Somebody cut the fence, damn it. I've been trying to figure out who did it, and I've tried to figure out why."

The smile left Gloria's face. "I'm sure that Lester did it." She squirmed in the car seat as she spoke and then explained, "He was on the way to one of his political meetings and was wearing a new pair of boots. You remember that it rained a couple of days ago?" Before Horace could answer, she continued. "There was mud where the road goes through the gate, and, well, you know Lester. He didn't want to get his new boots muddy. He probably cut the fence so he could drive through on the grass and keep his feet out of the mud. I'll bet that's what happened."

Horace just stood there with a look of astonishment on his face. "You're telling me that Lester cut the fence?"

"That's what I believe." She looked over to where Willis was back at work on the repairs. "I can see that he didn't fix it like he should have." Her face took on a worried look. "I'm sorry, Horace. Sometimes I don't understand the man I married."

"'It ain't your fault. It's just that some heifers got out, and five of 'em bloated and died on the alfalfa." He paused a moment and then added, "We got the rest back last night."

Gloria's face went white. "Horace, please don't tell Lester how you found out who did it. He can get mean sometimes." She pulled her arm back into the car and sped off down the road toward town.

Horace stood for a long time, his hands on his hips, thinking about his neighbor. Lester Shipton had to be about twenty-seven years old. Horace had been on the school board when Lester was a small boy, and he'd been a problem even then. He was intelligent and could be a winsome child. But he had a mean streak and would bully smaller children. He got along well enough in high school, although he was something of an outsider, and he graduated from the State College with a degree in agriculture.

Lester had only been home from college a couple of years when both of his parents were killed in a car wreck. He was an only son and inherited their twenty-five thousand acre ranch and its thousand head of cattle. He immediately began to act the part of a land and cattle mogul, much to the disgust of Horace and his other neighbors.

Lester developed a political ambition. He announced he would run for the state legislature when Joe Little, the incumbent, retired. There was arrogance in his manner, and most of those who were interested in politics thought that any opponent would soundly defeat him.

It was after he returned to the ranch from college that he met Gloria. She was eighteen years old, just out of high school and anxious to get away from a bad home in Illinois. Gloria answered an ad for a housekeeper on a ranch in Montana, thinking it would be exciting to go west. She ended up caring for ancient Mrs. McGuire, the most demanding and unyielding person that the valley had ever seen. Gloria tolerated the old woman's abuse for three months and then got a job in the grocery store in town. That was where Lester found her.

Gloria had the appearance of a heroine out of a romance novel. She was tiny. She had a perfect figure, and she was blessed with a fair countenance. Her long blond hair sparkled in the sunlight. All of the young single men in the valley hovered around her.

Lester had a certain charm and sophistication that she found appealing. He was six feet tall, muscular, with dark, handsome features. He dressed in tailored western clothes that fit his body perfectly. He wore an expensive watch and had a gold chain with a cross on it hanging around his neck.

Lester showered Gloria with gifts. He invited her to the ranch and impressed her with its size and with his importance. Gloria had known poverty and not wealth. Soon she was in love—either with Lester or with the ranch. It didn't really matter which. They were married two years ago at Christmas time.

Horace pushed his hat back and pondered her remark about Lester's mean streak. The old man wondered for a moment how they were getting along. But then he decided it was none of his business and went back to help Willis with the fence repair. They were just about to begin driving steel fence posts when Lester's Chevrolet pickup roared around the bend and skidded to a stop near the gate. He liked to brag that the pickup was 1974 new and candy apple red. Willis walked over to pull the gate open for him, as he had done for Gloria, but stopped when Horace gestured to him.

Lester opened the door to get out of his vehicle but shut it again when Horace started his way. He didn't roll down the window, but, instead, looked over at Willis through the windshield and gestured at him to open the gate

Horace wanted to discuss the dead heifers, so he grabbed the handle and pulled the door open. Lester turned a defiant eye to Horace and yelled, "Let go, old man. I've got things to do in town."

"You've got things to talk about right here." Horace's voice was calm but hard. "Five dead heifers, to be exact."

"I don't know anything about dead heifers. Now let go of the door so I can get going." Lester turned his head and yelled through the windshield at Willis, "Open the gate, damn it."

Horace reached for the younger man and grabbed the sleeve of his sport coat. "Listen here, Lester. You cut the fence and didn't fix it. A bunch of my heifers got through, and we found five of 'em dead in your alfalfa field. If you were paying attention to your ranch instead of making a damn fool of yourself over politics, you would have seen 'em too." He jerked at the sleeve. "Now, damn it, you're going to make it right, and you can start now by helping us repair the fence."

Lester pulled his arm loose, threw the pickup in gear, gunned the engine, and let out on the clutch. He probably intended to back up but that wasn't what happened. The wheels on the vehicle spun and drove it forward, directly into Willis. The youth was slammed backward and crushed between the grill guard on the pickup and the gate post. Lester stomped on the clutch to stop the vehicle from pushing on Willis. For a moment he just stared through the windshield at the young man in front of him. Willis gasped, and his eyes rolled back in his head. Then his body went limp and hung there, squeezed between the pickup and the post.

Lester ground the gears getting the pickup into reverse. When he finally got it going, he backed around and then threw gravel as he sped back the way he came.

Horace ran to Willis where he had crumpled to the ground. He started to kneel beside the boy to see if he was dead, but Willis was breathing and beginning to groan. Horace dashed back to his pickup, grabbed the mike to the CB radio, and called to his wife. "Mabel, can you hear me? Willis is hurt bad. Can you hear me?" All he heard in response was a lot of noise. So he tried again, yelling louder as though his effort would overcome the static. "Mabel, are you listening? Willis is bad hurt, and we need an ambulance. Call town and tell 'em."

A different noise that was more static than voice, seemed to acknowledge his message. He yelled it all again and added, "I'll head to town with Willis. Get Doc and the ambulance started." He couldn't understand her reply or even be sure that she had heard him. All he could do was hope that she got the message.

Horace ran back to Willis and found that he was conscious. The young man was rolling his head from side to side in agony. Horace stooped down and asked where he hurt. Willis couldn't reply for a while but finally groaned, "I think all my bones are broken."

"Which bones?"

Willis put his hand down toward his waist, tried to swallow, and then mumbled, "All of 'em from here down."

"Hang on. I'm going to get the pickup." Horace rushed to the vehicle as fast as his bowed legs and his high heeled boots would allow. He drove it in a wide circle to stop with the passenger door next to Willis. When he climbed down and hurried around the pickup, the boy was perspiring, his face was white as flour, and he was breathing in shallow puffs.

Willis's voice, when he spoke again, was a kind of squeak. "I think my guts are crushed. God, Horace, my belly hurts."

"Willis, I can't leave you here alone while I get help, so we've got to get you in the pickup. The box will be too rough riding so we'll load you in front on the seat somehow." Then Horace added, "Can you move at all?"

"God, Horace, I hurt so bad I can't do anything."

"Then I'll have to manhandle you onto the seat." Horace reached down and grabbed the boy under his armpits so he could pull and lift. He said, "Hang on Willis." Then he dragged the injured man around and leaned his back against the running board.

Willis let out a scream when he did it.

"I'm sorry Willis, but I don't know what else to do. We've got to get you to the doctor right away."

Willis was breathing hard, and sweat was pouring off his brow. "I'm really hurt, Horace. I'm not sure I can make it to town, even if you can load me up."

Horace sprinted around to the other side of the truck and crawled across the seat until he was looking down on Willis. "Can you stand it if I pull you up here?"

"Jesus, Horace, I don't know. Maybe you better just leave me and go for help."

"I ain't going to do that. You might be dead before I got back." Horace reached down and grabbed Willis under the arms again. "Listen, I'm going to drag you onto the seat and then you can lie down on the trip to town." Before Willis could say a word, he jerked and pulled the poor fellow up onto the seat.

Willis screamed in agony and then continued to whimper and gasp after he was lying on the flat surface of the seat. Horace walked around to close the passenger door, only to find Willis' feet sticking out. "Can you bend your legs so I can close this door?" Willis screeched at him, "Don't you move anything again. I can't stand it." After a moment he added, in a calmer voice, "No, damn it. I can't move my legs at all. Now don't touch 'em!"

Horace stood motionless for a minute and then remembered the steel posts in the back of the pickup. He got one, slid an end through the open window of the door, and braced the other end against the rifle rack behind the seat. With some old baler twine, he tied each end of the post in place to keep the door open and away from Willis's feet while they traveled. When the old man climbed into the driver's seat, he had to lift Willis's head and rest it on his thigh so he could get under the steering wheel. Willis didn't make a sound and seemed to have lost consciousness.

The road was rough and rocky as far as the lane going into Horace's headquarters. The pickup bounced around and the passenger door swung back and forth as far as the fence post would allow. Horace was afraid to go very fast for fear the door would come loose and smack into Willis feet and legs and injure him even more. He kept looking down at Willis, whose head was constantly jostled from side to side, but the young man's eyes were closed, and he gave no indication that he was aware of the world. Beyond the turnoff to Horace's ranch house, the county had graded the road. That allowed the old man to increase his speed a little bit, but no matter how careful he tried to be, Willis was still getting a mighty rough ride.

Horace spotted dust rising from a vehicle coming his way and hoped it was the ambulance. But the person driving the car that passed him was Gloria on her way home. She neither slowed nor waved as she went by. He wished she'd stopped so he could ask her to go to his place and call for help. With no one else in sight, the only thing he could do was keep on driving.

He had ten miles of dirt road and eight miles of pavement to cover to get to town. Fortunately the ambulance met him just before he got to the asphalt. Willis was still unconscious when the medics lifted him onto the stretcher and into the ambulance. They were much more gentle in moving him than Horace had been. Once he was loaded, they started for the hospital at high speed, with Horace following as fast as his old pickup could go.

When Horace reached the hospital, Willis was already inside the emergency room where the doctor and nurses were working on him. The old rancher used the hospital telephone to call Mabel and tell her that Willis was alive. Then he put his dirt-encrusted hat on the floor beside a chair and sat with his hands dangling between his knees while he waited. There was nothing else to do.

After about an hour, Doc Burns came out to the waiting room, still wearing green surgical clothes and with his face mask hanging around his neck. He pulled a chair over and sat down by Horace. "That boy has more broken bones than anyone I've ever seen. But he's young and they'll all heal. It sure will take some time, though." The doctor rubbed the back of his neck. "He's been bleeding internally, and I'm not sure what's going on in there. We need to get him to the hospital in Billings as soon as possible. I've called for a helicopter. They should be here any time." He looked sideways at Horace and asked, "What in the world happened out there, anyway?"

Horace told him how Lester had run Willis down at the gate. He added, "I'll be damned if I know what got into that man. He acted crazy."

"Well, Willis will probably survive but it's going to take a while. Does he have any family that should be notified?"

"Yes. His folks live in Big Timber. I'll call 'em right away." Horace got to his feet. "And I'll drive to Billings tomorrow to make sure that he's getting proper care. He's a good boy, and he's my responsibility. Damn!"

The doctor went back to the emergency room, and Horace headed for the telephone. Before he reached it, Sheriff Flaherty came in the door.

"Horace, your wife called my office a few minutes ago. Gloria Shipton's at your house all beat to hell. It sounds as if Lester really did it this time." The sheriff shifted his huge bulk from one foot to the other. "Mabel's bringing her in now to have the doctor patch her up." His feet shifted again. "I sent my two deputies out to the Shipton place to talk to Lester and get his story." He looked Horace in the eye and growled. "If that punk hurt Gloria, I'll do my damndest to see that he gets jail time. She's better than he deserves."

Horace walked back to the chair and sank slowly into it. He rested his elbows on his knees and his chin in his hands. "It's my fault. I shouldn't have jumped Lester the way I did about cutting that fence. I'm sure he beat up on Gloria because she told me that he was the one who did it."

The sheriff put his hand on Horace's shoulder. "It ain't your fault. Lester's always been a bully—when he thought he could get away with it. I have no sympathy for a man who would hit a woman. We'll take care of him when we get him in here."

The hospital clerk poked her head through the door and said to the sheriff, "You're deputy's trying to reach you on the radio. He said it's important." Flaherty mumbled, "Got it," and rushed out the door to his car and its radio.

Horace was still sitting in the chair when he heard Mabel's voice coming from the emergency room. He jumped up and met her as she came into the waiting room. His wife of forty years told him the story as they walked back to the chairs. "They're working on Gloria right now. She has a broken nose and lots of bruises but nothing more serious than that." Mabel sat in a chair next to her husband. "She told me that Lester'd been drinking. When she walked in the door, he started screaming at her because she told you he cut the fence. Then he just started beating on her. She finally kicked him between the legs and managed to get out of the house. That's when she drove to our place for help." Mabel shook her head. "The poor girl was sure he was following her, and she was scared to death. So I called the sheriff." Mabel looked at Horace as though she wanted his approval. He put his arm around her shoulder, and she continued. "Then I loaded her in our car and brought her here. I had your old shot gun with us to make her feel safe." She looked sideways at her husband again. "We didn't see nothing of Lester, though. I don't know what he did after she got away."

They found out soon enough. The sheriff started talking to them as he came back through the door into the waiting room. "Lester shot himself. My deputies found him lying on the kitchen floor with a six shooter in his hand. Put the thing under his chin and pulled the trigger. Plumb dead. Gloria was right. There was a whisky bottle on the counter." The sheriff shoved his hat back and rubbed his forehead with his forearm. "Horace, why in blazes would he kill himself? He was in trouble, all right, but it all could have been straightened out somehow."

Horace didn't say anything for a minute. When he did, he turned toward his wife. "Someone has to tell Gloria. I guess that's you and me, Mabel." When she nodded her head, they got up from their chairs together and walked hand in hand toward the door to the emergency room.

They sat with Gloria until the doctor suggested it would be best if she stayed in the hospital overnight. Mabel gave the new widow a gentle hug before they walked away. Horace held the door as Mabel climbed into their old Buick that was parked next to the emergency room entrance. Then he trod slowly back around to the front of the hospital where his pickup was parked. All the while he muttered to himself, "What a waste. What a needless waste. What a tragedy."

As he was reaching for the pickup door handle, the local machinery dealer walked up and put his hand on Horace's arm. "Glad to catch you. I did some repair work on a big tractor for Lester Shipton. A couple of days ago, I loaded it on my trailer to haul it back to his place. When I got to the fence between his ranch and yours there was a wallow of mud in the gate. I was afraid I'd get stuck if I tried to pull that heavy tractor through all the mud and water. So I cut the fence near the gate and drove around through the grass. There weren't any tools in my truck to repair the fence so I just left it." The man paused, dropped his eyes to watch as he kicked at a rock with the toe of his boot. He looked up. "I know I should have called and told you, but I just forgot."

Astonishment, then disgust, and finally cold fury darkened the old rancher's face. The dealer quickly moved two steps back. His eyes widened, and he put out his hands, palms forward, in an appeasing gesture. "Gee, Horace. I sure hope I didn't cause any kind of a problem by cutting that fence."

LEMONADE SPRINGS

I found the magazine while cleaning out the house after mother died. Two sheets of paper were tucked between the pages. One look and the memory came flooding back.

Will Hammer rode into the yard at a quarter to noon on May nineteenth, 1932. I remember the date because it was my eleventh birthday. I even remember the color of his horses. The one he straddled was dapple gray; the pack horse was dun colored. I wondered about a stranger who was traveling on horseback. This wasn't like the old days. Everyone had automobiles, for goodness sake.

The man pulled his pony to a stop at the gate to survey the scene. The two story main house, where I lived, was on the right side of a kind of quadrangle. The clapboard cook house was perpendicular to it in the middle and at the rear. The long, low log bunkhouse squatted on the left. Barns and other outbuildings were on the far side of the creek behind the bunkhouse. Tall cottonwood trees sheltered the whole compound from the wild, west winds.

After a moment's hesitation, the stranger dismounted. He led his animals to an old hitching rack near the entry gate and then marched in stiff steps to the front door of the house. The man appeared to be a bit bandy-legged.

Mother answered the knock. He quickly doffed his hat, exposing a shiny bald head, and introduced himself. In response to his question, Mother suggested he wait. The man nodded his head in acceptance and then passed the time on the front stoop by scanning the high hill to the north and the broad hay meadow to the east. When Dad arrived at the door, the stranger put out his hand, the hand that wasn't holding the hat. "Mr. Simon, I hear you need a rider."

Dad's eyes ran him up and down. Will Hammer was about five feet ten inches tall and had a muscular body. He was dressed in the clothing of any cowboy or ranch hand—cotton shirt, neckerchief, leather vest, denim pants, and high heel riding boots. Watching from the cook-house window I could see that everything about him was clean and neat.

"Well, I need someone to a do the summer riding—check the pastures and look after the cattle. Doctor any animals that need it. Call for help to do the doctoring, if that's required." He paused before adding, "And wrangle the work horses each morning before breakfast."

"Sounds like something I can handle. When can I start?"

Dad thought for only a second. "Right now, if you

want. The horse barn is over there. There's a small pasture behind the barn for your horses. It's the first wire gate to the left out the back door of the barn." Dad pointed. "Bunkhouse is over there. Cook house there. Dinner will be on the table in a few minutes. You can meet everyone."

"I'll be ready." The man turned abruptly to leave. Dad stopped him. "Don't you want to know the pay?"

"I'll take whatever it is."

The cook house had a long wide open room with the coal burning range against a wall at one end. A wooden counter ran most of the length of the back wall. A hand pump protruded through the surface of the counter near its end. A wide sink with a drain was next to the pump. One window overlooked the sink. A door next to the stove led to another small room with an ice box, cupboards, and shelves. Another door led to a tiny sitting room and, next to that, a small bedroom. A table with seating for fourteen—six to a side and one on each end— dominated the long room.

Will Hammer arrived at the cook house door just as the last of the ranch hands was trailing through. He entered in time to see each man pull a chair from a familiar place. Dad stood at the head of the table. Mother stood at the other end. My chair was next to hers.

Dad made the introductions. Pointing to Mother, he said, "You've met Eleanor." His finger turned to me. "That's our daughter. We call her Buzzy."

He then began to name the hands seated around the

table. "Meet Sam. That's Harry. And that's Luke."

As each name was spoken, Will Hammer nodded his head and repeated it. "Sam. Harry. Luke."

Last Dad turned to Auntie, who stood quietly near the stove, hands tucked under an apron. "My sister-in-law, Harriet Forsythe." He nodded toward the stranger. "Harriet, meet Will Hammer."

Auntie's face remained placid. "How do you do, Mr. Hammer."

The man bowed his head the slightest bow. "It's nice to meet you, Miss Forsythe." Another almost imperceptible bow before he pulled out the only empty chair from beside the table to begin the meal.

It took lots of horses to do the work at that time. About thirty work horses to power the haying and other equipment. About twenty saddle horses to use while doing the work with the cattle. All of those horses were in the corral well before breakfast the day after Will Hammer arrived—and each morning thereafter. And that day and each day thereafter, he saddled his own horse and rode out to check on the cattle. Thinking back upon it now, I wonder how he knew where to go—where were the boundaries of our ranch—where were the various bunches of cattle located within the boundaries.

Auntie was Mother's older sister—much older, it seemed to me at the time. That much I knew. About her, I knew little more. She had just been there, living in the cook house, from my earliest remembrance. Her body was rather square but of a pleasing form. No one would ever call her beautiful, but she had pleasant features. And she smiled a lot at me.

She and Mother shared the cooking duties, but Auntie did most of the work. I liked my aunt. She didn't treat me as a child, but more like an adult. She encouraged me to wear nice dresses. And she let me help with the work without criticism—only suggestions. I spent a lot of time in the cook house.

The cooking was done on a huge coal range. A coal scuttle rested on the floor near at hand. Each of the ranch hands was expected to take a turn at filling the scuttle. None of them liked the job. They apparently thought it was beneath a real man. So, too, with the wood box. None of them wanted to tote the split wood. Or tote the ice from the ice house. So Auntie frequently found it necessary to catch one of the hands as he passed by and ask him to fetch whatever was needed at that moment.

Then Will Hammer came. Not once after his arrival did Auntie have to ask for coal, wood, or ice. He hauled all of those things into the cook house on a regular basis. He stacked the wood neatly in the wood box. He not only carried the ice to the ice box, but emptied the drain pan at the bottom—without spilling a drop.

Auntie would stand aside when he arrived to do any of it. After the wood or ice was in place, she would always nod once and say, "Thank you, Mr. Hammer." No smile warmed the thanks.

He would nod, sober faced, in response. "You're welcome, Miss Forsythe." Other than that, they never spoke a word to each other.

Will Hammer seemed to take a liking to me. He smiled a lot and said I was cute. He soon realized that the one small horse among the rest was mine. A day came when he asked if I'd like to ride with him to check some heifers. I jumped at the opportunity. First, however, he went to the house to ask my parents if it was all right for me to do so. Dad agreed with an admonition to be careful. Fathers! Will Hammer threw my saddle over the back of Sunshine and held the animal 'til I was mounted. We rode together that day, and I rode with him from time to time after that. It was fun because he told me vivid stories as we traveled along.

One day, when we were returning to the buildings, he began to sing.

> *Come along boys and listen to my tale*
> *And I'll tell you of the troubles*
> *on the Old Chisholm Trail*
> *Come a ti yi yippie yippie yea yippy yea*
> *Come a ti yi yippie yippie yea*

His voice was deep and melodious. The tone and pitch were perfect. I asked for more, so he continued.

> *Started up the trail on September twenty third*

Started up the trail with the 2U herd

And then he sang the refrain once again.

As time went by I listened to the whole of the Chisholm Trail saga many times. Soon enough I learned the words and the melody and joined in the song as Will Hammer sang.

> *It's bacon and beans most every day*
> *I'd as soon be a eating the prairie hay*

In the middle of the housing quadrangle was a well and pump. Someone had long ago planted a couple of cottonwood trees nearby. Mother, who liked nice things, managed to get a small patch of grass to grow around the well. She also planted a few flowers to brighten the area.

It was a cool place to spend time during the summer evenings. Four benches provided resting places. The ranch hands often gathered there to tell stories and relax from the day's labors. Once in a while Mother and Dad would join them. Auntie never did. She listened quietly as she rested in an old chair on the cook house stoop. I, of course, had to be in the middle of any such activity.

One such evening, I asked Will Hammer to sing the song. His reluctance was evident, but Mother said, "Buzzy tells us you have a beautiful voice. Please sing for us."

What could he do? So I heard again the long lyrics

of the "Old Chisholm Trail." I almost giggled at this part:

> *My horse bucked me off at a creek called Mud*
> *My horse bucked me off round the 2U herd*

That evening I noticed for the first time that his chin rose slightly when he sang. And I noticed, for the first time, that his nose had a slight hook to it.

Once the others heard him sing, he was asked to do so whenever the group gathered. We heard the old western songs, "The Streets of Laredo," "The Strawberry Roan," and others. There were cheers and clapping after Will Hammer finished with each melody. I noticed that Auntie never joined in either the cheers or the clapping.

Once, as we were riding, I asked him to sing. He surprised me. Instead he began to recite.

> *Young Lochinvar came out of the west*
> *Through all the wide border his steed was the best*
> *And save his good broadsword he weapons had*
> *none*
> *He rode all unarmed and he rode all alone*

I listened in awe to Sir Walter Scott's ballad—all the way through to the end. So, at the next gathering, I asked Will Hammer to recite the poem for the others to hear. Once again he exhibited reluctance. And once again Mother prevailed.

> *But ere he arrived at Nertherby gate*

The bride had consented, the gallant came late
For a laggard in love and a dastard in war
Was to wed the fair Ellen of brave Lochinvar

My feelings at that point as an eleven year old girl? A silent, "Damn! Lochinvar should have started sooner and traveled faster." But then Will Hammer would continue with the recital toward its end.

One touch to her hand and one word to her ear
When they reached the hall-door and the charger stood near
So light to the croupe the fair lady he swung
So light to the saddle before her he sprung
'She is won! We are gone, over bank, bush and scaur
They'll have fleet steeds that follow, quoth young Lochinvar

That's when I always felt like cheering. Lochinvar had her, and the lovers were going to get away!

I looked at Auntie. Her countenance had never changed.

****

A dipper hung from a nail next to the sink in the cook house. One hot afternoon, Will Hammer carried a huge armful of wood to the wood box. After carefully stacking it, he turned to Auntie, hat in hand, to ask, "May I have a drink of water please, Miss Forsythe?"

She looked up from batter she was about to pour in a pan. "Of course, Mr. Hammer. There's the dipper—next to the pump." She dropped her eyes to go forward with the batter.

He drank deeply and returned the dipper to its hook. "Thank you Miss Forsythe. That was refreshing." Then he was out the door.

That may have been the longest conversation they ever had.

Once during the evening meal, Mother turned to the cowboy. "Will, we know you have land near Melstone. Would you tell us about it?" Everyone now called him Will—except Auntie.

He looked up from his pie, placed his fork on the plate, and leaned back. "Well, I have about two hundred cows and the land to run them. And I have a house that's set in some trees next to a small spring creek. There's running water in the house. I piped it from the spring up above. The house isn't large but it's comfy."

"Do you, by chance, have a picture?"

Much to my surprise, Will Hammer reached into his shirt pocket and pulled out a small snapshot. He handed it to Mother who peered at it and smiled.

"My goodness, it's a very attractive building."

The picture was passed from hand to hand. Eventually it got to Auntie. She seemed to spend more time than others in scanning every aspect of the house. At last she returned it to its owner without a word of comment.

He looked down at the photo for just a moment before stuffing it, once again, into his pocket. Before picking up his fork to finish the pie, he smiled and said, almost, it seemed, for his own benefit. "It's a tidy little place. I call it Lemonade Springs."

****

September approached and with it the loom of school. I hated the thought. Just before the first of that month, Will Hammer approached Dad one evening after supper. "I'll be leaving at the end of the week. Perhaps you could figure up my time."

Dad seemed non-plussed. "We had hoped you'd stay. There's still riding to be done."

"I know. And I don't like to leave. But my own livestock require care."

Dad wished him well when he picked up his check. Dad also told him he would have a job if he ever returned. Mother shook his hand. Auntie was standing in the door to the cook house as he led his saddled and packed horses from the barn. Seeing her there with her hands tucked under her apron, he paused and then tied the animals to the old hitching rack. With his hat once again in hand, he approached her. "Miss Forsythe, it has indeed been a pleasure to get to know you."

"Thank you, Mr. Hammer. I hope your ride home is uneventful." She didn't remove her hands from under the apron. She said nothing more.

I watched my poetic friend ride through the gate and off to the east with a broken heart.

****

Two weeks passed. I was back in school. When I entered the cook house upon my afternoon return from the school bus stop, Mother was preparing the evening meal. Auntie was not to be seen. In reply to my question, Mother pinched her lips and said, "Your aunt isn't here."

"Where did she go?"

"We don't know. She mumbled something I didn't understand, got on the eastbound train and left."

"When will she be back?"

"We don't know that either."

****

Now, long years later and looking at the material in my hand, I finally knew. *Ranch Romances* was the title of the magazine. The two sheets of paper were stuffed between a couple of the magazine pages near the end. In a column under the heading marked "Personals," one item was encircled in yellow crayon.

> *Former schoolteacher, age thirty-eight, never married, seeks a kind western gentleman to join her at the playground.*

There was no name. The return address was the magazine's drop box.

The smaller of the two sheets of paper had blue lines across it, as though pulled from a child's tablet. The handwriting was male and firm.

Dear Miss Forsythe,
    I'll travel up there and ask for the riding job. That will give you the summer months to size me up. I won't say anything to anyone about this. It's nobody's business but yours and mine.
        Yours truly,
        Will Hammer

The larger paper showed the neat feminine hand that I still remember as Auntie's.

Dear Sister and Brother-in-law,
    I'm at Lemonade Springs. It's a tidy little place. I won't be back.
        Yours truly,
        Harriet

JERRY BRAYED

The ancient cattle rancher dropped his sweat stained hat on the floor and lowered himself slowly onto the chair. Without looking across the desk, he placed his elbows on his knees and lowered his hands, knurled from years of hard labor, down between his legs. The man's once muscular frame was nothing more than a skeletal collection of bones. A faded flannel shirt hung from his shoulders as though draped over a scarecrow. With his head hanging down to expose his scalp, the few strands of hair he still retained appeared snowy white. They lay uncombed across skin that was marred by the brown splotches of age. For a long time he remained quiet while rubbing one hand against the other to relieve the arthritic pain that was a constant plague.

I pushed the legal papers I'd been reviewing to one side of the desk, leaned back in my chair and waited.

When he began to speak, it was with his voice directed at the floor.

"Many years ago—I was just a small boy at the time—my dad had a team of mules that he called Judy and Jerry. The mules had been worked side by side for so many years that they were inseparable. Even when they were in the pasture with all the ranch horses they were just comfortable in their own company. They didn't seem to need to be with any of the other animals.

"One night, when I was about eight years old, a horrible noise woke me from my slumber. It scared me so much I covered my head with the blankets. But then the noise came again, so I jumped from my bed and ran down the hall to the room where my mother and father slept. Dad, wearing only his underwear, met me at the bedroom door and took me by the hand. We walked together to the window that looked out onto the front yard. I stood on my toes and peeked over the sill.

"There was Jerry, standing close to the front porch of the house. When the mule saw us peering through the window he raised his head, opened his mouth, and poured out again the caterwaul that had frightened me so badly. I closed my eyes, put my hands over my ears and squeezed close to my dad. He patted me gently on the head, glanced out the window again at the mule and then back down at me to say, 'Something's happened to Judy. Jerry's come to us for help. I guess he thinks that people are the only ones that might fix whatever's wrong.' He rubbed his hand reassuringly through my hair and added, 'Go put your clothes on. We'll let Jerry lead us to his partner.'"

With his voice still directed toward the floor, the old

man continued, "I dressed as fast as I could and reached the back door just as my dad pulled on his boots and pushed a hat on his head. He took my hand as we walked to the pickup.

"Jerry had remained quiet since he'd seen us in the window and knew that someone had heard his cry. When he saw the pickup come around the corner, the mule headed away from the barnyard at a trot and on westward over the hill. We trailed along with my dad driving slowly to stay behind Jerry.

"Only one spring provided water for the animals held in the horse pasture. As we approached the spring in the dim light of dawn we could see the shape of something large, lying on its side. Jerry ran to the spot, looked down at the still form, then turned in our direction, raised his head and laid back his floppy ears. Once more, the mule rasped out that woeful cry."

The old man was silent for a heartbeat as though contemplating the remembrance. With a quick shake of his head, he whispered, "Judy was dead."

The rancher continued to rub his arthritic hands in silence for a long moment. Then he raised his eyes to look over my shoulder and off into the distance as he spoke. "Penelope and I have been married for fifty years. Our anniversary was last Wednesday." He dropped his eyes again to his hands and seemed lost in thought. At last he inhaled deeply and breathed out a long sigh. "I never was much for God and religion and things like that. But when Penelope took sick, I prayed to the Lord to make her better." When he looked up again there was a choke in his voice. "She died on Wednesday, our anniversary day."

A single tear appeared at the corner of his eye and trickled slowly down through a maze of deep lines and creases to the point of his chin. From there, the tear dropped silently to the floor. The aged rancher reached to the back pocket of his Wranglers and dragged out a handkerchief. He used it to wipe at his eye. With great deliberation he carefully folded the cloth and tamped it back into the pocket. Then he bowed his head toward the floor once again and slowly rubbed his brow up and down with the palms of both hands.

After a long silence, the grief stricken man inhaled again. His gaunt body shuddered as he released his breath. When he looked directly at me and spoke, his voice was a barely audible sob.

"Now I know why Jerry brayed."

MADIE'S AUTUMN FROLIC

Madie sat uncomfortably in one of the big chairs and scanned the reception area. It was more lavish than she could have imagined. The furniture was heavy and expensive. The carpet was so plush and deep that it seemed a shame to walk on it. Huge oil paintings adorned each wall. While Madie didn't recognize the names of any of the artists, she could tell by the quality of the work that each of them must be famous.

The receptionist, seated behind a wide desk, was busy answering the telephone. She wore a long dress the shade of burnt umber. It was accented by a silk neck scarf the color of a pumpkin. Madie envied her youth and her loveliness.

Only two other people were in the room. They sat in chairs, side by side, across from Madie. The man appeared to be about fifty years old. His pin-striped suit fit his large frame perfectly. His hair was carefully groomed and, Madie would have bet, the lustrous gray came from a hairdresser. His companion was much younger and wore a wedding ring. Madie guessed she must be his wife. The jacket and slacks that she wore were intended to flatter her figure, and they surely did. Her hair was long and blonde. There was gold jewelry hanging on her at every place it was possible to hang jewelry on a woman. The man sat with his legs crossed and his hands in his lap. The woman fidgeted and thumbed her way through one magazine after the other.

Madie glanced down at the plaid man's shirt she was wearing. At least it was clean. Her Wrangler jeans, also clean. Her boots, she realized, weren't as clean as they should be. Some remnant of the cow corral remained. Her attire was totally inappropriate for the surroundings, but she had an appointment and didn't feel she could leave.

The name on the letterhead said, "Sutherland, Coffman, and Blaine." She'd assumed they were three lawyers practicing together. It was a surprise, when she found their offices on the sixth floor of a tall bank building, to see the names of some thirty lawyers on the window panel next to the door. Now she felt intimidated by the surroundings, by the office workers who scurried across the room from one corridor to the other, and by the solemn silence that permeated the place. It was like a mortuary.

There were several fancy magazines on a low, flat table, so she reached for one to help pass the time. Just as she did, a nice looking man wearing a silk tie over a sparkling white shirt, but without a suit coat, came into the room and strode over to where she was sitting. He smiled at her as he said, "Miss Whittier? I'm Jeremy Blaine. It is nice to make your acquaintance. I've known your father for many years."

Madie rose from the chair, took his hand and mumbled, "Pleased to meet you."

With a wave, he indicated the corridor on the left. "Let me show you the way to my office." Then he added, "Would you like some coffee or a soft drink?"

"No thank, you. I'm fine." Madie wasn't fine. She was as nervous as a horse in a strange barn.

Jeremy Blaine led her down the corridor and into a huge office with large windows that provided a panoramic view of downtown Billings, Montana. A comfortable-looking chair faced his oversize desk. He held it as she settled in.

When the man was comfortable in his own chair facing her, he smiled and said, "I'm sorry about the death of your father. I hoped to attend the funeral services, but a court appearance prevented it." The lawyer shuffled some papers. "I understand that you worked with your father on the ranch."

Madie thought about that for a moment. "Yes, I work on the ranch."

"And I guess that you cared for him during his last illness. I'm sure that was difficult for you."

"Well, Dad died in his sleep. It was a blessing in a way, because he suffered a great deal at the end."

"Miss Whittier, how much do you know about your father's affairs?"

Madie thought again before answering. "The last couple of years I've written out checks so he could sign them. Checks to pay bills." She was silent for another moment and then added, "I have my own bank account. Dad would put money in it for my needs."

"Do you know the extent of your father's assets?"

"Well, I know he has the ranch and cattle. He has money in the bank." She shifted in her chair. "And there's the machinery."

"Miss Whittier, there is more than that. Over the years, your father saved and invested wisely. The last time he was in my office, about six months ago, he gave me an asset list. I've made a copy for you." He handed Madie several sheets of paper and then looked down at those on his desk. "As you can see if you look at the bottom line, Albert Whittier had a net worth of about eight million dollars. The ranch land is worth about three million— maybe more on today's market—and the cattle about three hundred thousand. He had about three million, five hundred thousand in stocks, bonds, and certificates of deposit. There is approximately two hundred thousand in machinery and equipment, in pickups, trucks, and automobiles, and in other miscellaneous items as well as cash in the bank. Most of that two hundred thousand is cash, savings, and checking accounts." He looked over his glasses at Madie to judge her reaction. When she just sat there looking back at him, he pushed the papers aside and began again by saying, "Miss Whittier…" He paused, took a breath, and said, "May I call you Madeline?"

"No one has called me Madeline since my mother died. You can call me Madie. That's what everyone else calls me."

"Thank you. And you can call me Jeremy if you wish." He leaned toward her with his elbows on the desk. "I know your mother is dead and that you are an only child. Your father wanted you to have everything, and he took some steps to get it to you with the smallest amount of death taxes. He made gifts of undivided interests in the ranch to you over a period of several years. That will all but eliminate the death tax." He looked down at some notes on his papers. "The small amount of death tax, if any, can be paid from his liquid assets."

He paused to allow her to comment, but she just sat straight in the chair, looking intently at him. "The cost of administration—the lawyer's fees—if you want us to handle it for you, will be about fifty thousand dollars." Again, he paused for reaction. When Madie merely sat mute with her hands in her lap, he added, "We could charge more than that under the law, but I believe that amount will cover our time and professional skills." Jeremy Blaine leaned back in his chair. "You don't have to retain the services of this firm to handle the estate just because I wrote the will for your father. You can go to some other lawyer, if you wish." He waited as Madie digested what he said.

At last she nodded and said, "No. I guess Dad must have been comfortable with you. And you know about his business. From what you've told me, I guess that I don't know much about it."

"Well, Madie, the thing that's important is that your father left you a wealthy woman."

Madie scrunched around in her chair and then rubbed her hands up and down on her legs. "How did Dad gather up that much money? We never had enough to fix up the house or even to buy good machinery."

"Your father used the old investment maxim, pay yourself first. Every time he received some money, no matter how small the amount, he invested a part of it before he used the rest to pay bills or to buy things." The lawyer leaned forward again. "Over the years the investments grew because he kept reinvesting the dividends and interest." He leaned back again and continued, "As you can see from the list of assets, there's a little less than two hundred thousand in his savings and checking accounts. That money will be available to you right away. You can use it to pay hospital and doctor bills, if there are any, and the funeral bill. You can pay the costs of administration as you receive the bills from our offices. Your father may have other bills that you must pay. But there will still be a lot of money for you to spend for anything that you need."

Madie looked at the list for a moment and then put the papers down. "I don't know what to do with that much money."

Jeremy Blaine laughed, "Your father hoped that you wouldn't spend it foolishly."

Madie straightened herself in the chair and asked, "What do we do first?"

In answer to that question, Jeremy Blaine launched into a long monologue about the administration of an estate. Madie listened with half an ear, but her mind was still trying to grasp the amount of money that her father had left to her. She heard him speak of appraisers and creditors' claims and filing fees and notices in the newspaper. None of it made much sense to her. But when she finally heard him say he would have papers for her to sign in three days, she knew the interview was over. As he walked her to the door of the offices, she thought to ask, "If I want to sell some cattle, can I do it?'

"Of course. Once you are appointed Personal Representative, you can sell anything want. And, as I said, the appointment will be made shortly after you come to my office to sign the papers."

Madie took his hand and thanked him. She headed down the hall to the elevator. As she came around the corner, she saw and heard the couple from the conference room in a raucous argument. The woman was using language that Madie only heard at the stockyard. The man had a firm grasp on her arm and looked like he was about to strike her. Their veneer of suave gentility was gone. When they saw her, they both immediately stopped and stood rigidly, side by side, while they waited for the elevator. Neither of them said another word while they rode with Madie to the ground floor.

As she got the pickup out of the parking garage, Madie decided that her apparel wasn't so important after all. The couple from the lawyer's office wore elegant clothing, but their words and actions told her that they were coarse and vulgar. And she probably had more money than they did. That thought amazed her.

****

She sat, the next morning, at the old kitchen table with her coffee cup in front of her. For the first time in years, she didn't start the day's ranch work right after breakfast. Usually it was a trip in the pickup or on horseback to check on the cattle, to put out salt, or to repair fence. This morning she was still digesting the information Jeremy Blaine had given her. Her father was dead. The obligation to care for him was gone. She no longer was tied to the ranch because of her father. And apparently she had enough money to do about anything she wanted. All of it was such a change that it was hard to comprehend.

Madie walked to the stove, poured another cup of coffee and then returned to her chair to think back over her life.

She had been pretty and popular when she was in high school. Her mother always told her that she should get an education and Madie assumed she would go to college. After graduation from high school, she enrolled at Montana State University. But then her mother died. Shortly before she was to leave for the University at Bozeman, her father asked her to stay home for one year. He said he was not used to life without his wife and needed time to adjust. So she did, thinking that she would continue her education the next year. But the next year he said he needed her to help with the fall riding because he had no reliable ranch hands. And so it continued from year to year until—one dark day—she realized that she would not be able to go to college at all.

She had dated a handsome and intelligent boy named Mike when she was in high school. He graduated from college with a degree in engineering and got a job with an aircraft company in California. Mike returned on vacation when she was twenty-five years old. He asked her to the movie and they spent time together for two weeks. The night before he left, he asked her to marry him and she accepted. They planned to be married in the church in Ryegate in one month. Madie was ecstatic and in love.

Her father had a heart attack the night she told him of their plans. He remained weak and bedridden long after the doctors said he should have recovered. Of course she had to care for him, so the wedding was put off. Finally the young man gave her an ultimatum. She must choose between him and her father. Madie cried all through the night, but the next morning she told the young man that she couldn't leave her father alone in his condition.

That was the last she saw of the man she would have married. Shortly afterward, her father recovered his health.

In the years that followed, she daydreamed about life as it might have been if she had married and had children. And she daydreamed that some other man would ride into her life and take her away. Madie watched *Love Boat* on the television and dreamed that she and some handsome man were sharing a cruise as passengers.

There had been one other man who was interested in her. He was a widower from Roundup and came calling, for a short while, about ten years ago. She enjoyed his company when they were together. When her father realized the man's intentions, he simply told her that he could no longer run the ranch without her help. If she left, he would have to sell it. And, he added, she must know how important the ranch was to him and how it would hurt him to let it go. So, once again, she sent a man away when she wished to do otherwise.

From then on the days went by, one after another, each like the last. She did the housework and also worked outside. The ranch was thousands of acres of grass and little else, so most of the work was with cattle, and most was done on horseback. She enjoyed riding and could do so with as much skill as any man. She sorted the yearling heifers to be kept for breeding from those to be sold. She roped calves at the branding fire. And, after a time, her father deferred to her judgment when they were buying bulls. The last couple of years, she had even negotiated the sale of the calves and weighed them at the scale for delivery to the buyer. Because the housework consumed a part of the day, her father maintained the fences and corrals until shortly before his death, so she wasn't burdened with those tasks. She remembered that he always spent money to buy the materials to keep the improvements, other than the house, in good condition.

But there was never any money for the house. From time to time, she had tried to get him to fix things in the kitchen. One burner on the electric stove was gone. She had a clothes dryer, but not an automatic washer. The refrigerator was old and didn't keep the food cold enough to assure that it wouldn't spoil. Again and again her father told her that they would have to make do. So she had made do. Now she wondered why.

Her piano and her books had sustained her through the years. The piano was old. Her mother brought it into her own marriage. Madie wasn't an accomplished pianist, but she enjoyed playing the tunes that were popular when she was young. The books came from the library in Harlowton or in Billings. She seldom dared spend the money to buy a book.

She didn't despise her father in spite of it all. He was a good man, well respected by everyone in the community. But the burden of caring for him at the end, when he was bed-ridden, had been difficult to bear. He was seventy-nine years old when he died, and it was time for him to go.

On her last birthday she was forty-seven years old. Now that she was no longer tied to her father or, for that matter, even to the ranch, she could do anything she wanted. But what did she want to do?

Madie put her cup on the table, wandered to her bedroom, and sat before the large mirror on the vanity. The woman that gazed back at her was still attractive. Her features were regular, and there were only a few wrinkles around her mouth and at the corners of her eyes. Her skin was burned by the sun and wind to the color of leather. Her caramel colored hair, cut short, had a sprinkling of gray.

After some meditation, she stood and removed her shirt and pants. She turned from side to side, while looking at herself in the mirror, to inspect every part of her five-foot, five-inch body. She ran her hands down her sides to her hips and noted that her waist was not as narrow as it once was. But she still had curves where curves are supposed to be. Every muscle was hard as a rock from the daily work. She was pleased that nothing, either at the top or at the bottom, showed evidence of sagging. Before she dressed again, she gave her backside a little shake. After a self-conscious giggle, she decided that she should still be of interest to a man.

But there wasn't any man.

It wasn't that she felt she must have a man to live with. It was just that the opportunity for a husband and children had passed her by, and she felt cheated. Through the years she had watched her friends in church and out shopping with their families. They had something that was denied to her. A part of that something was the love and appreciation of a husband. As she dressed, she thought about the *Love Boat* some more and wondered if a cruise would be as enchanting in real life as it appeared on the screen.

Her reverie was interrupted by a knock on the door that she knew would be Curt, the twenty-five-year-old son of one of her neighbors. He helped with the work while her father was dying and repaired some fence for her the day of the funeral. As Madie walked to the door to let him in, she realized that she must do something nice to repay him.

They sat at the table drinking coffee while he told her about the fence repair job and the additional work that needed to be done to make the fence secure. He paused as Madie refilled his cup and then began to tell her about the situation on the ranch—the ranch that belonged to his parents. He and his two brothers and their wives were all living and working there. "You know, I'm the youngest. And the ranch isn't big enough to divide among three of us when my parents are gone. There isn't even enough work to keep all of us busy now. That's the reason I like to help you when you need it." He looked at

Madie with a wry smile. "Edgar is the oldest. He always has to boss me around, and I'm tired of it." He swirled the coffee in the cup. "My wife and I are wondering what to do. Whenever I talk of going to town to get a job, my mother scolds me for not appreciating what my parents are providing." Curt turned in his chair and leaned his arms on his knees. "My wife is tired of it all, and I can't blame her. The other day she threatened to leave me if we don't move."

Madie certainly sympathized with the young man and told him so. She urged him to assert himself and make a life of his own. She didn't tell him her advice was based upon her own sad experience, but she supposed that he might have guessed.

After he left, she said to herself, "Well, I have no excuse now. I can start making changes in my life, and the place to begin is with my appearance."

****

The lawyer called and asked her to come to his office on Tuesday. She went through her clothes and decided that everything she owned, except for her shirts and blue jeans, was so out of style that she would be embarrassed to be seen in them. So she was dressed as before when she appeared at his office. She signed the papers that he presented to her and then asked, "You said I can do anything I want with my father's property. Could I lease the ranch? Or sell the cattle?"

"Yes, you can do either one. You can even sell the

ranch if you want to. But I hope you won't do anything like that, at least not for a year or two. You need to take time to accustom yourself to your new situation before you make serious decisions about your inheritance."

"I'm not going to sell either the ranch or the cattle. I just want to know what I can and can't do."

"Madie, as I said, you can do anything that you want with the property. It's yours once the federal estate tax return is accepted by the government and the tax, if any, is paid." He had a serious look on his face when he continued, "I have an obligation to warn you that there will be men who will learn that you have money and will try to take advantage of you. Such men can be very persuasive. I've seen women in your situation lose everything they have to some sweet talking scoundrel." His manner was intense. "Please be careful and, if you feel an urge to make investments or decisions suggested by a man that you have not known for a long time, please call me first. At the very least, I can check it out for you."

"I'll remember that—and take advantage of your offer." She paused, and then added, "If the occasion arises." Madie turned to leave and then looked back over her shoulder with a smile. "But I don't think any man can sweet talk me out of very much."

From there she went to the ladies clothing store that she saw advertised in the paper. She intended to buy some clothing like that worn by the receptionist in the law office but, after she looked at and tried on several sophisticated suits and dresses, she changed her mind. That kind of thing just wasn't for her. At the large western store, where she occasionally bought riding gear, she tried again. A very pleasant and attractive woman, about her age, brought out carefully tailored blouses, skirts, vests, jeans and jackets that fit perfectly and flattered her figure. She added several brightly colored accent pieces and asked that everything be wrapped and delivered to the Northern Hotel.

Then she went to a salon. It had been years since she had been in a beauty parlor and never to a salon. The proprietress was waiting and was prepared to give her the complete makeover that she requested. It took hours, but her appearance, when she looked in the mirror, made it worthwhile. She was still the same Madie, but now the worn ranch look was gone. It was replaced by a feminine and slightly sexy appearance. Madie liked what she saw.

Her final stop was at a jewelry store. She intended to buy gold, but decided that silver complemented her hair color and complexion. She bought necklaces, bracelets, earrings, and a jeweled watch.

At her room at the hotel, Madie dressed in one of the new outfits—light gray, form-fitting slacks, snow white blouse with a rose colored scarf at her throat, and a dark gray vest.

She was ready to face a new world.

As she walked to a table in the dining room, other patrons turned to look as she walked by. The new world liked what it saw.

After dinner, she stepped into the bar, took a stool—one away from the door—and ordered lemonade. The bartender frowned at an order that didn't contain booze and was not gentle when he placed it down in front of her. It spilled on the bar, and she had to be careful not to put her elbow in it. Madie swiveled on the stool and looked around the room that reeked of cigar smoke.

There were two couples, about forty years old and obviously friends, seated at one table. Two older men, dressed in rancher's clothes, were huddled at another table. One of them was smoking a cigar. When the tough looking, bleached blond barmaid brought them another drink, he reached up under her skimpy skirt and patted her on the bottom. She neither slowed in her work nor even looked at him.

She just muttered, "Hands off, Buster."

Three other men of indeterminate age sat at a table in the back. By looking in the mirror she could see them size her up as she sipped her lemonade. Finally one of them rose from his seat and climbed onto the barstool next to her. He had a huge belly, a bulbous nose, and an odor like a brewery. He was puffing a little from the exertion of getting on the stool when he said, "Hi there, Sweetie. Can I buy ya a drink?"

Madie swung around away from him and shook her head. "I'm meeting my husband. He's getting a haircut downstairs." She scurried out of the bar as fast as she could without running.

Two days later, while riding along on her favorite horse in a pasture far north of the ranch buildings, she reflected on her attempt at barhopping. It was a certainty, she concluded, that she wouldn't find the companionship she wanted by looking in a saloon. She could never picture herself on the *Love Boat* in the company of the drunk with the bulbous nose and bulging belly. Perhaps she should move to Billings, join a church, and get involved in other activities that might attract men of the right age. Or go on one of the singles cruises that she saw advertised in travel magazines.

But what of the ranch? She had no intention of selling it. What else could she do with it if she was to be gone for long periods of time? Then she thought of Curt. Why not lease it to him? That would accomplish two things. It would assure that the ranch received proper care, and it would allow Curt to begin a life away from the others in his family. She owed him, anyway, for all the help he provided at a time when she really needed it. The further she rode and the longer she thought, the more she liked the idea.

Back at the house, she called Curt's number on the telephone. Kate, his wife, answered. "Kate, this Madie. Can I come to your house to visit this evening after work?"

"Why sure, Madie. We're always glad to see you. What's up?'

"Oh, nothing. I just need to visit with you and Curt

for a few minutes. I'll see you about seven." When she hung up the phone, Madie thought how lucky Curt was to have such a wonderful young lady for a wife. It made her idea even more appealing.

****

Coffee cup in hand, Madie looked first at Curt and then at Kate. "I'm thinking of leasing my ranch. Would you folks be interested?"

"Gee, Madie. That's a surprise. Just yesterday Kate and I wondered if we should ask my uncle, Otis Starke, if we could lease his ranch. He talked about leasing once a year or so ago." He frowned and added, "But we haven't any cattle, machinery, or money. How can we lease any ranch?"

"Well, I don't know about Otis, but I'll lease you my land, and you can run the cattle on shares. I'll even finance you to get you started, if that's what it takes." Madie leaned her elbows on the table. "I want to do it because I know you'll take care of the ranch. You'll run it right. Why don't you talk it over and call me. If you're willing to take it on, I'll have the lawyer draw up the papers."

Curt looked at Kate who was silently nodding her head. When he looked back at Madie, his mouth split into a wide grin. "Kate and I don't need to talk it over. We'll do it. It's an opportunity we never thought we'd have."

Now it was Madie's turn to grin. "You've got it."

She stuck out her hand to seal the deal. Then she asked, "What about Otis?"

"Gee, I don't know if he was even serious, but one time he mentioned that he would like to be able to get away, now that his mother's died. He doesn't say much, but I think he might like to travel. You know—see the world, take in the art museums and concerts. Otis likes those kinds of things."

Curt furrowed his brow, squirmed in his chair, and continued. "You know, the ranches would work great together. He has hay and not enough range. You have range and no hay." He turned to Kate. "Honey, maybe we should talk to Otis about it. Can't hurt, I guess."

Madie said, "You're right about that. It can't hurt. I think you should talk to Otis." Then she rose from her chair, hugged Kate, and went to the door. "I'll call the lawyer about our deal tomorrow. We'll get it done as soon as possible."

Outside the door, standing beside her pickup, Madie said to herself, "Otis! Why haven't I thought of Otis?"

The trip home in the pickup gave her time to think about him. Otis was a senior when she was a freshman in high school. He was tall and slender and played on the basketball team. He also sang in a quartet. The girls all thought he was handsome, and he had lots dates. But he was studious and quiet. After graduation, he went back to his parent's ranch and kind of disappeared. His father passed away not long after that. Otis kept on ranching and was seldom seen in town. Madie knew that he had cared for his mother until she died a couple of years ago. It surprised her that she never realized that she and Otis shared a common experience.

He would be about fifty years old now. The last time she saw him was at the post office some six months ago. He was still slender and walked straight and tall. His hair was white, but his face was still attractive. The thing that she remembered the most clearly, however, was his dress. He wore the shirt and Wranglers that were customary, but they were spotlessly clean and were even pressed. His broad brimmed hat was perfectly shaped and lacked the sweat stain that impregnated every other western hat in Golden Valley County.

At the post office, he spoke to her and, when he did so, removed his hat. She thought the gesture to be gentlemanly, almost courtly. Not many men did that nowadays. Looking back, she wished she had done more at the time than nod and smile when he said hello.

But that could be remedied and she would start tomorrow, right after she called the lawyer about her deal with Curt and Kate.

****

Her hand trembled a little as she picked up the phone, and she scolded herself for acting like a scared teen-ager. "Otis? This is Madie Whittier. Could I visit with you some time about your nephew Curt?"

"Why of course, Madie. I would enjoy a visit."

"Well, how about I come to your place tomorrow morning about ten o'clock."

"That would be fine. I'll have the coffee pot on."

"See you in the morning, Otis."

"I'm looking forward to it, Madie."

Otis lived on the river about a mile off the highway, east of town. Madie had never been to his place and was surprised to drive up to a house that had obviously received constant care. The grass in the yard was green, even though it was near the end of September, and it was carefully groomed. Fall flowers were growing in all the right places. It hardly seemed like a bachelor's abode.

She looked at herself in the mirror once again before she got out of the pickup. Today she was wearing form-fitting jeans and a colorful blouse, not too flashy but intended to accentuate her figure.

Otis opened the door, and she found herself standing directly in front of him. She had forgotten how tall he was. It almost cricked her neck to look up at his face. He must be six foot two.

Otis smiled a warm smile, grasped her hand, and then stepped aside to allow her to come in.

The large living room was as immaculately maintained as the outside of the house. The furniture was not new but was solid. An entire wall was lined with books. And in the corner was a magnificent grand piano.

"It's nice to see you again, Madie." He gestured with a wave of his hand. "Let's go out to the kitchen. It's more comfortable there." Otis held a chair for her at the large table and then poured coffee in two cups—not mugs, but china cups.

A small china plate held fresh baked sugar cookies, and there appeared to be more on a cookie sheet covered by a white linen cloth. The smell made her hungry, even though she had eaten her usual big breakfast. *My goodness,* she thought, *he knows how to bake.*

After some pleasantries, Madie told him of her intention to enter into a lease agreement with Curt and Kate.

"Otis, do you think that they can make it? If I lease them my ranch?" she asked.

Otis smiled as he answered, "They're really good kids. Curt knows cattle, and Kate's willing to work hard. They'll make it if anybody can."

Madie only half heard his answer. She was noticing that his teeth were straight and white. The skin at the corner of his eyes wrinkled nicely when he smiled. While his hair was pure white, it was thick, and a shock of it kept falling onto his forehead. Madie's eyes sparkled when she spoke again, "Curt mentioned that your place and mine would work well together. You have hay and I have grass."

"Why, I guess that's right." He chuckled and looked her right in the eye. "You can't be suggesting we partner up, because you already told me you're leasing your place to Curt."

"No, Otis. That's not quite what I had in mind. Curt thought you might consider leasing to them too."

"The truth is, Madie, I have thought of it some. I've enjoyed ranching and don't want to sell. But it would be nice to be able to get away and do some other things." He took a sip of coffee and then put the cup down and looked across at her. "Is that what you're thinking, now that your father is gone?"

"Exactly. But I'm not only thinking about it. I'm going to do it."

"Well, let me consider it. I think a lot of Curt and Kate. I'll talk to them about it"

"Jeremy Blaine is the lawyer that's handling Dad's affairs. I told him to draw up the papers for the lease." She hesitated before adding, "He thinks I'm crazy." Finally, she said, "If you decide to lease to Curt and Kate, you might ask him to do the legal work. The agreements would then be about the same."

"That's interesting. Jeremy is my lawyer too." He smiled that warm smile again. "I'll tell him that you're not completely crazy." There was silence for a moment before Otis observed, "We seem to have some things in common."

Madie rose from the chair and said, "We do indeed, Otis."

On the way through the living room, Madie stopped, looked at all the books, and commented, "You must read a lot."

"I like to read—history, current fiction, the classics." His eyes twinkled when he added, "I tried to read *Moby Dick*. It was too much for me."

"Who could really read *Moby Dick*? Most people just pretend they've read it." She turned to the piano and asked, "Do you play?"

"A little. I enjoy music." He sat and ran his fingers up and down the scale in a brief arpeggio. Then he sat for a minute, and Madie thought he might play something like a concerto by Chopin. Instead he ran through the opening of Basin Street Blues, putting a funky twist to the melody. His laugh, when he stopped, was self-conscious. He even blushed a little. "I'm not much good at this."

"Otis, I'm a lot worse. But we'll try a duet sometime." She shook his hand at the door and started to walk away. She looked back over her shoulder. "There's a concert at the Alberta Bair Theater in Billings on Friday. Would you like to go?"

Otis's eyebrows rose in surprise, and it took him a moment to answer. "Why yes, Madie. You bet I'd like to go. I'll call to see if I can get some tickets—if you'll go with me."

"I've got the tickets. And I'll call you later to make the arrangements."

As she walked away, he called after her, "Madie, you sure look nice."

"Thanks, Otis. I'm glad you noticed."

****

Madie didn't want to sound like she was giving orders, but she had plans. "Otis, park at the curb in front of the hotel, and we'll unload the bags. Then I'll check in while you go around to the parking garage." She smiled across at him. "The theater's only a couple of blocks up the street. We can walk to the concert."

She was standing at the elevator when Otis arrived from the garage. They rode in silence to the seventh floor. Down the hallway, the bellman unlocked a door and stood aside to allow them to enter a small sitting room. Otis had a puzzled look on his face. Madie answered the question he was about to ask. "It's a three room suite. That seemed to be the most convenient arrangement." She motioned toward the doors that led into the two bedrooms. "Which one do you want?"

Otis was looking uncomfortable. "Why I don't care, Madie. You take your pick." He handed the bellman a five-dollar bill to get the man out of there. For a bachelor, talk with a woman about bedrooms was bad enough without a stranger listening.

Madie carried a small bag into one of the rooms and indicated that Otis should bring her larger one. He did so, put it down quickly and hurried from the room. Madie looked at his back and grinned. He was kind of cute in his embarrassment.

She dressed in a light blue silk blouse and a long

dark blue, flowing skirt. Her silver earrings had tiny spurs dangling from them. Several silver bracelets encircled one arm. The makeup was just enough to accent her features. A final look in the mirror confirmed she was ready.

Otis stood in the sitting room when she stepped through the door. She almost gasped at his appearance. He was dressed in a dark gray single-breasted suit and wore a vest over a starched white shirt that had faint gray stripes. His tie, perfectly knotted, was of a lighter gray than the suit and was patterned with barely discernible red characters of indistinct shape. He wore shoes—brightly shined black shoes—not boots. He was gorgeous!

The hostess fawned over them as she led them through the dining room. Every eye in the place turned, as they moved along, to appreciate the strikingly handsome couple. Madie was aware of the looks of admiration and with a small inward smile, thought, *By golly, we deserve it.*

Otis's manners were perfect during dinner, and he was an easy conversationalist. He was attentive to Madie's remarks and demonstrated quiet good humor. They finished dinner and walked arm in arm to the theater. Their appearance was as much a hit at the theater as it had been in the dining room.

Both were enthralled by the music and were quiet and content on the walk back to the hotel. Otis surprised her by suggesting an after theater dessert. The dessert was consumed in easy conversation about the music. Otis surprised her again by suggesting a small liqueur to follow the dessert. Otis was more sophisticated than she had expected.

Then it was time to return to the rooms.

Madie removed her clothing as quickly as she could and slipped into a filmy silk negligee. It was almost, but not quite, transparent. And it was short, so short that her fingers, hanging at her sides, were below the hem. She covered it with a longer silk robe, looked in the mirror again, and walked to the door to Otis's room. She took a deep breath and walked in—without knocking.

Otis was sitting on the bed, facing away from her and reading a newspaper. His shirt, shoes, and socks were off. He looked around at her over his shoulder and inhaled sharply. Madie smiled a tenuous smile and said, "Hello, Otis."

Otis slowly folded the paper, got up from the bed, and put it on the table. He looked at Madie for a long time and then sat back down on the bed facing her. He put his elbows on his knees with his hands clasped between his legs. With his head down and his eyes on the floor, he spoke in such a low tone that she barely heard him. "Madie, I've never been in bed with a woman." He looked up at her out of the corner of his eye and then back down at the floor. The back of his neck glowed a bright red.

Madie stepped close to him and rubbed her hand across his shoulders. There was a lot of muscle there. Then she stepped back and whispered, "Otis, I've never been to bed with a man. It's time we corrected the situation." She slowly removed the robe in the way they described it in a romance novel. After she dropped it on the floor, she cocked one hip to the side and smiled at the man on the bed.

Otis looked up and jumped to his feet while reaching his arms toward her. "My God, Madie, you're beautiful!"

****

Madie woke up at five-thirty in the morning, as she always did. She lay with her eyes closed for a minute or two and then looked over at Otis. He was wide awake, lying with his hands behind his head, staring at the ceiling. She snuggled over next to him and put her head on his shoulder. He dropped his arm down to pull her close and asked, "Madie, have you ever thought of going on a cruise?"

She snuggled even closer. "I've already made the reservations, Love." She blew gently in his ear. "We sail from Miami a week from Tuesday."

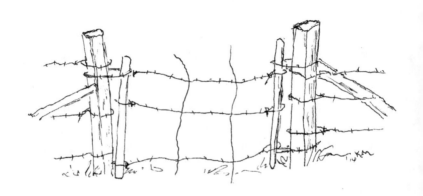